RUNT

Niall Griffiths was born in Liverpool in 1966 and now lives in Wales. He has published five novels: *Grits, Sheepshagger, Kelly + Victor, Stump* and *Wreckage.*

ALSO BY NIALL GRIFFITHS

Grits
Sheepshagger
Kelly + Victor
Stump
Wreckage

NIALL GRIFFITHS

Runt

VINTAGE BOOKS
London

Published by Vintage 2008

2 4 6 8 10 9 7 5 3 1

Copyright © Niall Griffiths 2007

Niall Griffiths has asserted his right under the Copyright, Designs
and Patents Act 1988 to be identified as the author of this work

First published in Great Britain by Jonathan Cape in 2007

Vintage
Random House, 20 Vauxhall Bridge Road,
London SW1V 2SA

www.vintage-books.co.uk

Addresses for companies within The Random House Group Limited
can be found at: www.randomhouse.co.uk/offices.htm

The Random House Group Limited Reg. No. 954009

A CIP catalogue record for this book
is available from the British Library

ISBN 9780099461159

The Random House Group Limited supports The Forest Stewardship
Council (FSC), the leading international forest certification
organisation. All our titles that are printed on Greenpeace approved
FSC certified paper carry the FSC logo. Our paper procurement
policy can be found at www.rbooks.co.uk/environment

Printed and bound in Great Britain by
CPI Bookmarque, Croydon CR0 4TD

Last summer it was not like any other summer of my life it was when so many things happened to go Crash in my head. When I said tara to the school and laughed and did a dance on my own and NotDad pushed me out and up to Drunkle's house because He Needed Me they said, Them Two, He Needed Me is what They said cos Auntie Scantie was found up in the tree like they found the ripped sheep but *she* wasn't ripped or not in a way that could be eyed and he's lonely They said and He Needed Me but They were going to Go Their Separate Ways and wanted me gone, My Mam Bethan and that dark bastard NotDad. And he said oh yes comen stay did my Drunkle after the men in white suits with guns had come to shoot all their sheep, his and Fay's, even if there was nothing wrong with their feet *or* their mouths they just shot em all blam anyway around that tree that Auntie Scantie Fay climbed and then jumped out of necktied to a branch and where after that they found the ripped sheep too or maybe that was another tree I can't remember it, which one. And oh yes Arthur died too, that dark face-scrapey fella falling back into the mountain with my good dog Arrn gone now but I remember him always I remember looking through his eyes. Yes that Arthur went that man who was Not Of This World and *his* wife didn't climb a tree but she did make me go flying before her fingers went away but go flying different to when I have My Times which I *did* that summer with Fay and them Lordy fellers and the Everything-thing and the peagreen planet in space. *Fits* some people like *teachers* called them and My Mam Bethan as well and NotDad called them something else not right and cruel cos he's like that and I don't know where he is now and don't care either cos I never flippin did. But My Times I call them and Drunkle does too and there was some of Them last summer, and as well there was lots of things dying and going away and I heard Snowball the bull who'd been dead for a long time in the byre and he was shot too that time long ago which I didn't and don't remember cos I was small then. And I still hear Arrn calling me but I miss him awful and last summer there were Stones and a Beast that no one saw like I didn't see the Bala monster and haven't ever and there was *lots* of things last summer and some of them I like, they happy me still but some of them days still dark me dark me like the hole Arrn and Arthur went into or like the Bala Lake I watch on Drunkle's screen. But one thing I remember big and of a mostness was the My Time I had and usually I don't remember My Times cos I *can't* remember them only the quickness and quietness before I fall into Them when I can watch Crow walk and hear a dinosaur roar as He walks and then I go somewhere where I *feel* a nothingment only as if the God in Crow or in that Tree or in them Stones that Drunkle so loves has got down in the mud and is kneeling on my neck.

★ ★ ★

I danced when I left the school, left that stupid school. It was raining and I danced in the raininess at the bottom of the playground by the ditch and the other boys laughed but I didn't care I was in a gladness to be gone, dancing by the ditch where I used to watch frogs and once saw a snake *eat* one of them frogs, his webby feet still kicking out of the snake's mouth and the snake going all big with the frog inside. Laughed they did them boys to see me dance but I didn't care cos I was Free and gone away from teachers and all them walls as well and after I'd done my dancing I *ran* down the lane and into and through the town and into my garden and had a play-fight with my dog who is called Arrn cos that's the sound he makes when he growls which he only does to those who are *afraid* of him and I'm not *afraid* of him he is my dog and I love him and he loves me I love very much his redsome ears. He wanted to follow me into the house but he couldn't cos he always has to stay outside even in the rain coming down, even in the snow coming down cos NotDad says he is dirty and doesn't like him cos he says his name at him and when I went in that same NotDad looked away from Mam and at me and Mam was sitting at the table in no food smells and she had her face in her hands and NotDad was above her his face red but not like Arrn's ears were red and he put a Looking on me with his face in his swinging head and then turned away again to show me his back and he spoke:

—Aw Jesus Christ. Get him away, Bethan.

My Mam Bethan put a sob into the room.

—I mean it. Get the little fucking freak away or he'll get the same. You *know* I'll do it, kid or no kid.

My Mam Bethan told me to go upstairs behind her hands and I heard her voice all wet and thick and shakey like the green jelly we used to have on Sundays and NotDad shouted something suddenly which made me and Mam jump and made Arrn bark outside and Mam told NotDad that she'd call somebody who could come and pick me up and she took her hands away from her face and one of her eyes looked like the blackbird's egg I found one time that had fallen from a tree and smashed and the tiny bird inside all blue and bulgey with bursted veins and reddy-yellow stuff everywhere and swollen, that's what My Mam Bethan's eye looked like. And red hot I became then and I jumped on that bastard NotDad I ran and jumped at him all red hot I was but he caught me by the neck and I couldn't scream any more so Mam screamed for me and he threw me outside where me and Arrn made our plans to get him one night and kill him like the buzzards kill mice. I saw it happen in my head-ness, Arrn taking NotDad's throat in his teeth and shaking his head like he does when he catches a rat up at Drunkle's farm where then I couldn't wait to be, away from NotDad and My Mam's eye. We sat in the old useless car which had no wheels and had gone all flakesome-brown for the shelter in it and we made our Plans to murder that bastard NotDad and we laughed when we imagined him dead and then felt better about Our Worlds, me about *this* one and Arrn about the one he is from which I don't know about. Arrn always makes me feel better. But I'd just left school For Ever and shouldn't've *needed* feeling better but that bastard who one day will be Dead and

Gone always makes things dark, always puts a great big sick on me and we sat in that stinky car me and Arrn like being inside a drum it was with the rain on the roof and we made Our Plans and the sound of that rain on the rustsome roof like a drum started to make me go somewhere in my selfness, kind of that drifty feeling just before everything disappears in My Times, like that drummy noise was drawing me into it and away from *me* or pushing me somewhere like all the old waters in my head were being swirled around by the noise and I couldn't do anything but watch that swirling and there was nothing else in the world *but* that swirling which is how It happens most of the time, how They My Times come upon me. But behind all that drumming I heard Drunkle's truck pull up outside and I heard him go into the house and I heard some shouting, two men and a lady shouting, and then Drunkle came out of the back door and he stood in the rain looking around for me and smiled when he saw me in the car, he did, put a big smiling into the rain when he saw us, me the driver with passenger Arrn. Drunkle came over not walking very properly and leaned into the car and I was happy'd by seeing him. I could smell his breath and the pubs in it cos he's my Drunkle.

—Shwmae then. Off for a drive, is it? Didn't know dogs could drive these kind of cars. Maybe a Rover, eh?

He laughed and rubbed my head and Arrn's too and Arrn wagged happy cos Drunkle has no fear for him either which is what Arrn likes.

—Want to come for a drive with me? In *my* truck?

—Where to?

—My house. You like it there.

I pretended to think about it for a bit but I don't know why cos I knew the answer would be yes. I do these things sometimes, these pretendy things and I don't know why only that they happy me in small ways.

—Can Arrn come?

—*Course* he can, bach. I've got a beef knuckle he can have, take him til Christmas to get through.

—Okay then.

Arrn wagged and wagged and wagged his tail. I wagged happy too in what felt like my tailbit just above my bum but I don't have a tail so I must've been wagging somewhere else.

I like going to Drunkle's house. Liked it for as long as I can remember cos it goes up away, away from the town and NotDad who never leaves the town nor does My Mam but she *wants* to and she's *tried* to but she always goes back. I like going up and up and up into the cloudy green-nesses which sometimes I can't see cos of the mist which floats out of that upness like steam coming out of porridge or tea or the hot bread-and-milk that Drunkle makes me sometimes for breakfast. I like the big birds in that upness that move in T-shaped shadows through the thicksome greysome air like floating crosses that Jesus was nailed to and I like the whitesome bits of snow that you can see up here even when it's sunny in the down-belownesses and the hares and the foxes and the badgers at night-time and everything else, this is not the same world

6

up here as the one in the belowness and I like it best cos of its highness and the voices I can hear up here when no one is talking and I like it when I look in the mirror of a lake and see the ends of my strawy hair all blue cos of where they've been dipped in the sky.

Drunkle drove slow cos he was my Drunkle. Sometimes I thought he was going to drive through the fence and we'd roly-poly all the way down to the bottom of the valley and be bashed dead bad all three of us. Arrn was making a whining in the back seat a bit scared he sounded which he never sounds cos he is from Another World where he has always been King.

—So, yur auntie, Drunkle said. —My wife. *Ex*-wife. What d'you think about never seeing her again?

I couldn't answer his question. Because I thought that I *would* see her again somewhere and even if I wouldn't what could I say to Drunkle about how I felt about it? Drunkle asks these questions all the time. He will take me up to a High Place where people long ago planted a Big Stone in the ground and he will ask me how I feel about that Stone and I will just look at him standing there in the rain and mudment as still as That Stone and I won't know what to say to him or to the Stone. And Arrn will wag his tail at the Stone as if it is his friend and come to pat his head or give him food.

—You know what happened, aye?

I nodded, cos I *did* know; men in white suits with guns came up here and shot all the sheep and after they went Drunkle's missis my Auntie Fay jumped out of a tree still attached to the tree with a rope round her neck. Drunkle himself found her the next morning after he'd been looking all over the High Parts for her in darkness and storminess and he cut her down with a knife. Her name was Fay but I called her Auntie Scantie sometimes in my head cos once when she was drunk she rode a horse through marketday Llanybydder wearing only her scanty underwear and all the women shouted I bet and I bet as well that all the men hid parts of themselves but didn't turn away cos she had a way of making you feel burning hot, my Auntie Scantie Fay did. All the men hid parts of themselves and never turned away from her when she was around, they did, all of them always did.

—Every last one of em, Drunkle said. He was drinking from a bottle with one hand and driving the wheel with the other. —Shot them all. Perfectly good animals, every last one. Me and Fay, we would've known if something was wrong and all's they had to do was quarantine us for a bit, cut the road off, y'know . . . Foot-and-mouth virus can't live moren a hundred yards outside of a host, did you know that?

Yes I did I said but I don't think he heard me cos he just went on talking and driving and having a drink from his bottle. We passed some trees and the sunlight through them trees flashed and then FLASHED in the truck and I started to feel happy and going, that taken-away feeling and every tiny creature in these woods I knew, every animal from deers to things the size of a full stop and even smaller I knew by name and I knew their lives and what they did and what made them live and what would kill them but not whether they were good or bad cos every last single one of them was Good. Even the spiders and even the lice and the owls with their claws and the stoats with their jaws and moving ways like the oil that comes when Drunkle drains sumps and their murdering of the baby rabbits and the grown-up rabbits too and even them horrible orange flies that make their homes in poo, all of it all of Them was nothing but Good and I felt my eyes roll back to look at my mind and then Arrn licked the back of my ear cos I think he was a bit scaredy of Drunkle's swervey driving and his tongue's warm wetness brought me back into the truck and Drunkle's talking and I was gladded and I reached back and stroked Arrn, happy'd by him for bringing me back cos I wasn't really ready for My Times just then and I never really am. But I knew them all, I did then, every crawling flying jumping sliming spitting biting thing up here in this High Earth place.

—How could I have known, Drunkle said in questiony words altho they were not a question. —How could I have known . . .

His face was all of a wetness. I don't think he was talking to me really but his bottle and his truck and the upness and mist around him that he drove us through to his house.

—Fucking compo. As if *anything* could make it better, as if *anything* could ever compensate. Having to take your own wife down from a tree. Not all the money in the world, mun, not every last penny in the entire fucking . . .

And then I got a bit of a shock cos in a sudden he

9

smiled all big and grabbed and shook my knee in his hand all big too and lumpy like a turnip.

—Still got *you*, tho, eh? Still got my special nephew, isn't it?

I gave the smiling back to him. —And Arrn.

—Oh and Arrn, aye, mustn't forget old Arrn. Us three, we'll get through it all together, won't we? Us three, boy, we're an army. Aren't we? Nothing can touch us three, isn't that right?

I nodded and said yes and I liked the feel of my knee in his hand but I liked it better when he put his hand back on the wheel cos then the truck wasn't going All Over The Road any more with the big big drop beside. I liked as well very much the army of us three me and Drunkle and Arrn, our own little army in the world against people like bad bad Arthur and NotDad and them who would shoot a feller's sheep or a lady's sheep too and make that lady turn herself into fruit. I *liked* being in that army and I felt happy then even tho the sheep and Auntie Scantie were all Dead and Gone and My Mam had a bad egg eye cos of NotDad and I was still burning red hot at NotDad but I was happy too with Drunkle and Arrn in the truck, our army of three up here in the High Parts.

—Yur special, boy, you know that? Yur not like other boys. There is in you a peculiar place . . . *diff'rent* place . . .

Uh-oh, I thought; here we flippin go. Drunkle was starting to talk in that Strange Way he does when there is enough drink inside his belly to make his words go Strange and not like he normally speaks or not like anyone normally speaks. And being up here too with the world so far below sends his speaking strange and he makes words that I can never understand but sometimes they sound nice like when he calls me Special and things like that but his words do go all funny and he gets a kind of torch in his eyes as if he is seeing a world different to this one where everyone speaks like he does and it is not Strange to speak that way like him.

—A peculiar place that only you can go to and one other but that one other is everything. D'you understand me? There is a wound in you where He can enter. D'you understand what am saying?

I couldn't hear the big 'H' that Drunkle put on his 'He' but it was like I could *see* it. Like a giant rugby goalpost standing out all of a whiteness on top of the green mountain with Drunkle's little house below it that I could now see.

—Your wound is a doorway.

—I'm not cut, I told him. —He just grabbed me on the neck, he did. I'm okay. Don't worry, Uncle.

He laughed. —You're not cut in your skin, no. But see in here?

He thudded the bottle against his chest.

—And in here?

He clonked the bottle against his head.

—*That's* where yur wounds are. Them Times you have, you know when you go away from everything? That's your wound, that's where you're different to other people. It makes of you His favourite, His chosen vessel among the millions and why should you be so? Why should you have this burden put on you?

Them big H's again. Two of them this time but

going quick away cos we drove close up to Drunkle's house then and the top of the mountain was now too steep to see.

—Cos yur a healer. Hear me? You were put here to help others in their pain. People like you have been around since we first started living in caves and realised that that orange flickery stuff the sun made in the dry grass could be all we needed in the world, the, this, the *physical* world. People like you, aye, but not *many* people like you. Because . . .

He stopped his speaking and I was glad because he was speaking things I didn't know and didn't want to know really cos I wanted to get out of the truck and into the house and Arrn did too, no rest in him on the back seat there with his claws click-clicking at the windows and his whining. Drunkle drank from his bottle and looked out at the mountain rising up in no noise except for the engine ticking as the truck fell asleep and then he looked at me and he grinned.

—Teatime, anyway, isn't it? What d'you fancy?

Eggs I wanted, two of them fried like suns.

—Then eggs it is.

We went out of the truck and Arrn like a mad thing ran across the muddy yard and I went to go shouty at him to come back but Drunkle said no.

—Don't bother, bach. He's as happy to be away from that place as you are. And no more sheep for him to worry no more, is there?

That made me sad. No more sheep making their noises up here, none of them any more like little clouds on the sides of the mountains. No more lambs when the sun starts to come out for the year moving like springs in the fields with their eyes all big and ears all floppy.

—Will you get any more, Uncle?

—What, sheep?

Nod.

—Don't know for sure, but probably not, no. Couldn't, really, not with Fay being gone and all that. I mean, they were *her* sheep, really, all this was her idea. Her inheritance money that bought this place. City girl too, she was. Never thought all this could get in her blood, like, but . . . Suppose it must've done.

His face had gone wet again and he shook his wet face and then whistled for Arrn who came running to us with his feet and his face all dirty with bits of straw sticking up out of the muck on him like he had grown yellow spikes. I noticed then that it smelled a bit bad up here and it never used to smell bad and that it looked all dead untidy and it never used to do that either with bits of machines everywhere and empty barrels and stuff and plastic bags blowing across the yard in the breeze. It used to be clean up here and it wasn't now was what I was thinking but I still loved being up there in the High Bits with my Drunkle and my dog and that NotDad bastard was far away in the Belowness. My Mam's bad eggy eye was down there with him, far away.

Drunkle threw his empty bottle away into a pile of mud against the midden wall like a drifty bit of snow but black and smelly and it sank in and went squelch as it did. Then he opened the door to his house and all three of us like a great little army, me the soldier and Drunkle the general and Arrn the High King, all went inside.

—Do you know what it's like?

Two fried eggs I ate from Drunkle's own chickens like two little suns on my plate they were. Arrn got given a beef knuckle and he was chewing it and crunching on it for hours with bits of it everywhere but Drunkle's house was such a bad mess anyway and it never used to be that way that more mess didn't matter any more.

—Do you want to know what it's like?

Drunkle was drinking from another bottle and that's all he had for his tea, no food. And he was doing it again, again he was putting questions at me which I couldn't make an answer to so he answered them himself.

—It is like fear. It is like being very, very scared. It is like being lost in a forest somewhere at night-time and something is stalking you through the trees. You can't see it, so you don't know what it is, but from the sounds it makes you know that it's very, very big and could with ease and pleasure rip all your arms and legs off and you know that that's *exactly* what it's going to do *when*, not *if*, it finds you.

I didn't like that. Big thing of evilment hunting me in the woods and me all alone then me with no arms or legs screaming and no help coming I did not like that no and I went to put my hands over my ears to keep out Drunkle's words but I knew that he was needing me to listen to him and that he'd be made sad if I hid my ears with my hands. So I looked at Arrn instead but he was still bloody busy with his knuckle holding it tight in his mucky paws and bonebits like little spears all around him there on the dirty rug in front of the fireplace where a chair burned like *I* burned at the thinking of that Stalking Thing.

—It is the dread of death, and the terrible fear of my own aloneness. It cripples me utterly, being alive and alone, being without Fay. No man should *ever* have to cut the body of his suicided wife out of a tree. No one should *ever* have to suffer that. How can a man live, after doing that? How can he?

At it again with his questions he was.

—How could I have known . . . how could I have known . . .

At it again with Them Words he was and at it again he was with his eyes all melty like the springs in the High Parts when the winterness goes. And he was at it again too with his bottle-gulpy ways but he's always been at *them* cos he's my Drunkle.

—Everything's gone to a mess. See the mess around here? Lonely people become first untidy then they become filthy cos cleanliness loses its point and we yearn for distractions and letting the shite build up is exactly that and d'you want to know why? Because then, see, then, you can *clean* everything up. Just got to hope that the urge to clean comes on you before you get buried in the muck, isn't it?

He showed me his teeth in what looked a bit like a smile.

—That's the race, boy, isn't it? To beat the shite before it buries you. Cos that's what it wants to do, see, it wants to creep up on you and suck you into it. Big mound of black stinking shite from the earth's bowels and —

Drunkle then made a terrible sucky sound and I thought uh-oh ear-hiding time again but again I didn't and Arrn had his tongue inside his bone now. His ears looked very bright red in the light from the little flames from the burning chair.

—I'm gunner have to get some stuff from your mother, aren't I? You gunner be up here all summer and everything, you're gunner need some medicine. You're still on the lamotrigine? That sodium valproate?

I did not know the second name only the first one so I gave just one nod and then one shake of my head. Drunkle told me to hold my hand out so I did and he held it for a moment then sat back going 'mmm' like he thought he was Dr Llewellyn in the town who I once liked but hadn't seen for ages not since NotDad came into my life which was when I stopped taking the pills too which didn't really matter cos My Times just sick'd them back out anyway.

—No shaking. Have they put you on clonazepam?

Nor did I know that name as well so I shook my head. I wanted those names to stop.

—I'll have to have a word with your mother.

Funny eyes in my Drunkle again there was then. Little fires in them from the burning chair or his burning brains I didn't know but they turned his words again and there wasn't much left in his bottle.

—See, my Drunkle said putting a looking at the flames. —There is no God in happiness. When yur happy, see, there are claims and demands made on you

16

and these can seem to you like interruptions, like a distraction and an undermining of your contentment. They're not wanted in laughter. When two people laugh together, they don't need a third voice butting in because that weakens their unique togetherness. But, see, when yur in pain? Well, then you go to Him for comfort and all's you find is an absence. The fucker's not there. All there is is silence.

Like the bit of nice silence then that came into the room when Drunkle stopped his talking but I knew it wouldn't be for very long only the pops of the chair in the fire and the crunching of Arrn at his bone. And a noise in my ears maybe my heart pushing the blood up into my head and I wanted that Quiet to go on I wanted to go up to look at Bala Lake on Drunkle's screen and wait for the monster. I went to ask him if his screen was still showing Bala Lake but he carried on with his funny talk looking now down into the nearly empty bottle as if the little hole in the top of it was a little ear he was talking into. A little round glass ear.

—She speaks to me, y'know. As do all the dead to all of us. You've got to learn to listen to what the dead say because they have tales to relate and lessons to teach us. All the dead everywhere in the earth beneath your feet in the thin soil. Listen to what they're saying.

Glug glug and another bottle was empty. I saw the lump in Drunkle's throat jump up and down as he made the bottle go empty with his head back over the back of the couch.

—Remember the chrysalis we watched last summer? Remember when it hatched and the butterfly came out?

I went nod cos I did. The butterfly came out like a wet thing like something you'd spit out at school dinner cos it was yacksome and then it opened its wings and it was like something else, something dead different to anything yacka. And then it became even better when it flew away and that was the best thing about that summer maybe even the best thing ever or one of them anyway.

—Well, when the chrysalis was empty, when the butterfly had gone . . . *that's* what my body is now. Her death is a shock to my body; this thing I live in was once the body of her lover and now it isn't so it is completely different to me now. I don't recognise it. I don't even *like* it any more. I don't want to live in it any more. So do I just wait? Or do I follow her? But if I did she could be broken even further and she wouldn't want me to do it. But if she can observe my sorrow then she knows that there's nothing she can do to relieve it so her purgatory is made worse, always worse. There's nothing either of us can do, now, and we did everything we could for each other when she was alive. Except for at the end, when she was alone. Completely and utterly alone.

He drank again from his bottle even tho it was empty so he just drank the air inside it and I was glad cos it made him stop his Words. Putting a big sad in me them Words were and I remembered my Auntie Scantie making a cake for me the summer before it had cherries in it and I remembered her too taking me for a ride on a horse around the lower field I sat between her legs with the horse's big brown neck between mine and it was great to be between that

18

horse and my Auntie and I remembered the two warm-
nesses around me and Auntie Scantie's arms holding
the reins and driving the horse around the field and
I felt her pressing warmness against my back and I
went all hot as I did then but in a different way cos
never again would I ride on a great big horse around
a field with her laughing and pressing all warm behind
me. I remembered the smell that came out of her hair.
I liked my Auntie Scantie. She made men stare and
hide parts of themselves but it was me she took up
on to the horse and I'd never ever see her again and
that thinking shoved Sad into my body.

The phone rang as Drunkle got up out of his chair.
He picked it up and spoke and I could tell then that
it was My Mam Bethan cos he said her name. They
spoke for a bit and I tickled Arrn's head but he wasn't
interested in me cos his bone was better but he didn't
growl at me and say his name at me cos he never did
but he will say his name at other people even go to
bite them sometimes but never me or Drunkle cos he
liked both of us and we liked him.

Drunkle passed the phone to me. —Here y'go, bach.
Talk to yur Mam.

He went off into the kitchen and I heard him
opening another bottle and I talked words with My
Mam. I said hello and she said how are you are you
okay and I said is *he* still there and she said it was best
if I stayed where I was For The Time Being cos they
were Going Their Separate Ways and *he* didn't like it
and anyway I loved it Up There didn't I? Yes I said I
said I was happy and didn't tell her my sadness about
Auntie Fay and Mam said do I need my tablets and

I moved my shoulders up and down but thought then that she couldn't see me do that moving over the phone so I just said mmm and she told me that I'd been fine recently, she *told* me that and didn't ask me it and I wanted to tell her that no I hadn't but I didn't cos she Had Enough On Her Plate and did not need more worryness but I did not like that her Telling Me and not Asking Me and she said that we'd be good company for each other me and Drunkle and I said mmm again even tho I love my Drunkle but he can talk strange things and she said he needs the company now doesn't he? And to Keep An Eye Out for him but I didn't know what that meant and thought it would hurtly blind me halfways. She told me that I was sixteen which of course I knew and that I was now a Man which I didn't care if I knew or not cos men were either bastard bad people like NotDad or Arthur or not happy people like Drunkle and I didn't really want to be like none of them even if I did love my Drunkle I didn't want to be like him in his not-happy ways. And she told me to keep in touch and that she'd come up to the house and see me next week and we could go for a walk and I said okay which meant I know you won't come and she told me to look after myself and Arrn and Drunkle too and she told me that she loved me and I said okay and she hung up and her voice went and the telephone then went brrrr.

—How is she? Drunkle asked, back on the couch in his place with another bottle. I did the shoulder-up-and-down thing again which this time could be seen by the person I was doing it at and Drunkle did not answer with words or with anything else which was okay cos the shoulder-up-and-downy thing wasn't a question anyway. Drunkle just looked at me. I didn't want him to start his talk again so I asked him if I could go and see Bala Lake and that made him put a smile at me and we went upstairs to the room which I slept in and he turned his computer on and it made a wheezy-whiny noise and clicked and purred like Drunkle's cat that lives in the barn and is called Charlesworth and is fat like a furry rugby ball and had just had kittens which I wanted to see but not just yet cos they were too tiny still and Charlesworth would hiss and swipe. Drunkle made the arrow move across the screen and then after a bit of time I could see Bala Lake on the screen with the words 'MONSTER WATCH' in red at the top of it. Just the water of Bala Lake all dark and still and I got an excitement in me and got a bit jumpy inside cos of the monster that might come out of the lake and Drunkle laughed and said no one's seen it yet but he knows a feller who reckons he saw it one day when he was in a rowboat fishing on the lake and that it was like a great big crocodile with hooves which Drunkle had told me before but he told it to me again then cos he was my Drunkle. He said he didn't believe this feller but I did cos I wanted to. And we sat and watched Bala Lake for a bit just me and Drunkle. He drank and watched the darksome waves on the screen and I did too except I didn't drink but I could've had an orange juice if I'd wanted one or some lemonade but I didn't. Arrn came up to join us but he didn't watch too he just took his beef-bone under the bed and went on crunching it in the dusty dark under there and me and Drunkle didn't see any monster but I was happy there like that and I think he was too, just us two sitting there in a togetherness like that and not talking or anything just watching out for monsters.

Drunkle put his head to the side like birds do when they're listening or maybe they're not but Drunkle was.

—Can you hear an engine?

I listened with my head straight up and could.

—There's a truck coming up the mountain Drunkle said and I thought flippin heck My Mam was quick and not telling fibs either. Drunkle went to the window and pulled a curtain back and looked out and the engine-noise got bigger. It got bigger and bigger until it was dead loud and a light came into the room and swooped a slice of yellow across the walls and Drunkle said:

—Aw Christ. It's Arthur.

Fall then fall went my heart inside, once cos of who it *was* and then twice cos of who it *wasn't*. I heard a shouting outside and then a banging on the door down below, the door to the house.

—I'll go down and see what he wants. You stay here and if you see the monster be sure to call me up, eh?

He gave a smile to me but looked worried and the door-banginess went on til Drunkle went downstairs and opened it and then I heard a big, big shouting:

—FUCKING BASTARD! MORE DEAD FUCKING EWES! SOME CUNT PAYS THIS TIME BOY NOT ONE WORD OF A BASTARD LIE!

A growling came from under the bed in the dusty dark. I heard Drunkle say:

—Shh, mun, shh. I've got the boy upstairs. The nephew.

—THINK I CARE? THINK I CARE WHEN ANOTHER FUCKING EWE –

A door banged shut downstairs and then I could hear the shouting only through the floor and not proper words just a loud, loud voice. Arrn growled again from under the bed and I told him it was okay so he went back to his crunching.

But it wasn't okay, really, and Arrn probably knew that which was why he went 'arrn' and said his name. Cos nothing was ever okay when Arthur was there to make it not. I was more scared of Arthur being downstairs in the house than I was of seeing the monster on the Bala screen cos Arthur was a kind of monster himself who liked to hurt people. He was always hitting people and he had a wife who he would hurt and a daughter in my class at school before school went away who had a terror-ness in her for him but of course she wasn't in my class any more cos there was no school any more which should've been happying me but it didn't cos of NotDad and Mam's eggy eye and now Arthur with his big shouting down-stairs and I was scared for Drunkle. Some people there are, some fellers who are born with a black thing inside them as black as Bala Lake and just as sad as that and that's Drunkle and there are others who are born with another kind of blackness inside them that wants to put hurtings on others and make a kind of blackness in them as well and that's Arthur. He's a scary man. I thought he might hit Drunkle and then come up and hit me too but then I thought that Arrn would rescue me and bite his bastard head off but that thinking couldn't make me laugh that time like it normally did cos Arthur was too big and shouty and angry all the time and the only time I saw him smile or heard him laugh was when I saw him hit people like he did that time a summer ago when I was outside the Farmer's Arms waiting for Drunkle and feeding birds with crisps and Arthur came out with another man smaller than him and I hid in a bush and saw Arthur hit the man and the man fell and then Arthur stamped on his face lots of times and before he went back into the pub Arthur scraped his boot on the sharp edge of the step like I do when I've trod in dog poo and it made me think that the man's face was to Arthur like dog poo is to me and that put a big big sick into me. I wanted to go and see if the man was okay but I had too much scaredness in me and sickness too and after a while the man crawled off. And Drunkle came and got me and we drove home and I tried to tell him about what Arthur did and the poo-facey stuff but he just told me to hush and told me that there are not many people in the world like Arthur and that in fact Arthur was probably from Another World and not this one cos *I* was from this one and *Arrn* was from this one and *Drunkle* was from this one and *Bethan* was from this one so how could Arthur be too? And I remembered that then behind Arthur's shouting but it didn't stop me from remembering that poor man with his face scraped off and Arthur's wife in the shop with her arm in a sling and Arthur's daughter in the school with her face all black and one time her arm in a sling too and she said she fell off a horse but no one

believed her cos we all knew what Arthur was like
even the teachers but they didn't say anything cos like
everybody else they were scared of Arthur too.

Arthur should live in Bala Lake. Arthur should be
That One in the darkness and the slime. Maybe he *was*
the monster from the lake come out to hurt people
no big croco-horsey thing but a horrible thing shaped
just like a man big like a bull standing up on its back
legs with red hair and red beard come up out of the
deep blacksome water to eat people in his way. I wished
he'd go back there, I did. Or if not the lake then some
hole in the ground or cave somewhere or something
where no one could be hurt by him any more cos
that's the world he comes from not this one with me
and Arrn and Drunkle in it that Arthur comes from
a Different World one dark and far away in a beneath-
ness and he should go back there I would be gladded
if he did that very very much.

Bala Lake just lay flat and darksome with the moon
on it shining and I watched it for ages. Sometimes the
wind would make the webcam wobble and it would
be as if the lake not the camera was moving from side
to side but it wasn't really that. It was too dark to see
the mountains on the other side of the lake and all I
saw was the water of the lake like all the other times
I'd watched it and no monster but there *could* be a
monster and that thinking happy'd me in a way and
there *was* a fox, tho, skinny fellow come down to the
lake for a drink and then went away again and that
happy'd me loads seeing the fox like that having a
drink. I told Arrn about him cos he and the fox are
brothers and Arrn lay on his side under the bed with

his head sticking out from the darksome dusty under-neathness with all grease and bonedust on his face and he looked at me as I spoke to him and listened to me as well because he was understanding every word I said even tho he's a dog cos I can speak his own Special Words and he can speak mine too.

Arthur stopped his shouting but still he went on talking in an angerment that I could hear coming up through the floor. He was like a war. I could hear my Drunkle's voice too much softer than Arthur's trying to make Arthur's voice softer like his which after a while it did but not as soft as itself cos there was still an angerment in Arthur and always was and would be. Arrn fell asleep with his face all side-pressed to the floor cos he was listening to the voices too and his ears moved flickery and so did his tail but he didn't do that flat sideways running thing that he does some-times when he's in sleep. And a scary thing happened cos it was like a blacksome mist come up drifting through the floor from downstairs and it was like the badness of Arthur trying to find me like the stalking thing Drunkle made His Words about before and it swirled around the room all inksome making a kind of hissy sound like the snake that swallowed the frog but I wasn't sure if it was Really There or not even tho it was dead dead scary but Arrn didn't wake up and I hid my eyes with my hands and counted to forty-nine all slow and when I looked out again at the room that blacksome mist had gone and I was gladded by that very much again.

I started to feel sleepy then and wanted to be in sleep like Arrn was but wanted to wait for Arthur to go so I'd feel safer and better. But I must've fallen asleep anyway cos when I woke up I was floating through the bit of air between Bala Lake and the bed and I landed all gentle on the bed cos Drunkle had laid me on there light as a leaf falling to the ground in the autumn times that I like very much cos of the colours. And he was very drunk my Drunkle was cos when he went to sit on the edge of the bed by me he nearly missed the bed and when he spoke his voice was like a stream being tripped up by the rocks under it.

—Arthur's gone, he said but it sounded like this: *Thurzzgn.* —He's mad about finding another dead sheep. This time up a tree. Twenty feet up in the branches all ripped open like the others. Tried to blame it on a dog but what dog climbs trees?

No one else in the world could hear Drunkle's Very Drunk Words it would just sound like noise to them but I could cos he's my Drunkle. He rubbed his face in his hands and it made a sound like the sound I get when I scratch the pig's back with a stick outside in the yard.

—Someone's been keeping a lynx or something as a pet and it's escaped or they've let it go, that's what it is. No mystery. No Alien Big Cat or anything it'll just be someone's escaped pet.

I thought of all the murdered sheep on the High Parts found ripped into bits and then I thought of a lion out there on the darkest tops of the mountains roaring at the moon over a dead sheep all blood on his face and in his mane or a tiger in the trees just waiting. Those thoughts made me go funny inside me

not like a badness or like My Times but like
something nearly good. I didn't like the dead ripped-
to-bits sheep but I *did* like the thought of the animal
that made them that way if lion or tiger was what it
was or even lynx or wolf or anything else like that.

—So Arthur's arranged some kind of . . . *expedition*.
Tomorrow. A hunt, like. We're gunner be camping out
for a day or two.

He rubbed his face again and made that pigscratch
noise again then he rubbed my head and it made a
different noise not really a noise at all only in my ears
and not the room.

—So get some sleep, bach. Early start in the morning.

He rubbed my head again and Arrn's too nearly
falling over cos he had to bend then he went out of
the room and closed the door behind him. I heard
him go down the stairs and then I heard him make a
noise through the floor as if he was having a cry then
I went and brushed my teeth and turned Bala Lake
off and then I took my clothes off and got into the
bed. I slept for a bit and then woke up with a thirsti-
ness in my neck so I went downstairs for some water
cos everyone knows you Shouldn't Drink From The
Bathroom Tap and I saw my Drunkle asleep on
the couch all curled up and one fist pressed to his ear
like a shell, as if in his sleepiness he wanted to hear
the sea. I drank some water and went back up the
stairs and got back into the bed and lay there slotted
into the darkness with Arrn snoring underneath me
and I liked it, being there like that. I listened hard til
my ears stretched out and could hear all the sounds
outside of the house like the wind and the small raining

and the owls going screech and a lady fox doing that noise that lady foxes do, that screaming noise somewhere in the trees or on top of the mountain next to the moon and I liked it, liked it all. I liked knowing the owl and the lady fox by name. I liked very much knowing every raindrop by name and liked it too that the owl and the lady fox and every last bit of rain knew my name back as well.

It wasn't proper light when I woke up but I was awake enough as if it was. I lay in the bed all warm for a bit and listened to the noise of no wind cos it had gone somewhere else in the night-time-ness but there was still a raininess outside, just a bit. I reached down over the edge of the bed and my fingers found Arrn's furryness and tickled it and he stood up and looked at me all happy'd with his tail going wag so I got up and got dressed and went downstairs to the kitchen and Arrn followed me. The couch had no Drunkle on it cos he must've woken up and gone to bed so I drank some milk and gave Arrn some too and then I ate an apple and went out into the morningness.

I liked Drunkle's High Place farm but it was sadding me a bit then cos there was no Auntie Scantie Fay on it and it was all under a messment with barrels and bags everywhere and lots of machines gone all red-rusty and mud and muck in pools and heaps everywhere and it never used to be like that and as well there used to be sheep but there was none then just two pigs which I scratched at with a stick and they closed their eyes cos all pigs like stick-scratchings. Pigs are my friends. They know me, pigs do. Arrn liked them too, cos he stuck his nose through the bars and one pig touched it with *his* nose like they nose-kissed and I liked seeing that it made me laugh a bit. Ooo, Arrn fancies Mrs Pig. Then I went back outside and went into the barn and climbed to the top of the strawbale hill and looked out across the other proper-er hills and saw them in the mist and the sun coming up bright and big birds calling in the mist that was lifting off the mountain and I felt so happy to see it but of a sudden a bit sad too cos I could see down the valley that the Town was in and thought of Mam stuck with bastard NotDad in the house. But then I felt better again cos I looked away from that valley to the top of the biggest mountain which was glowing cos a bit of gleamy rock up there was caught in a sunbeam and it glowed like gold up there on the sky and it happy'd my heart parts inside. I pointed at it for Arrn to look at too but he thought I'd thrown something for him so he bounded off the straw hill and looked up at me from his new belowness and I laughed then he saw something run across the yard and he ran off after it into the byre and it was prob-ably a rat.

I heard someone say 'mmrpknaow' and I looked around and saw Charlesworth behind me in the straw with her paws folded to her chest and resting on a little platform of straw and I laughed cos she made me think of a shopkeeper with his elbows resting on the counter of his shop like Mr Lewis in the Town who sells me sweets. I asked Charlesworth for a pint of milk and a bag of sherbet lemons and she looked at me. Then I stroked her head and asked if I could see her New Babies and I was waiting for her to hiss at me but she didn't and behind her in a hole of darkness she'd made in the straw I could see the tiny kittens moving and Charlesworth stood up and started to butt me with her head going 'prrr prrr' and I could then see the kittens and they were so small. Their eyes were open but all kind of gummy and they had tails like tiny furry points and when they stood they rocked from side to side like my Drunkle does sometimes and they made sounds so squeaky-high I could hardly hear them with my ears. They were all tiny but one of them was the tiniest and coloured black and white and the others were kind of reddy with white bits and I picked this one up and it didn't weigh much more than the air I held in my hands with it and Charlesworth gave me a little growl but that's all she didn't swipe or hiss just growled a small growl and watched me with her eyes all green. The kitten was so tiny with an angryness in its scrunched-up face too big for that tiny face too big for that tiny body and it made a noise I didn't really hear then bit me on the thumb and wouldn't let go and as it bit me it poo'd too but I didn't mind the pooing or the biting in fact I *liked* it, the biting not the pooing, cos it didn't hurt and I thought that I was Arthur or even better NotDad and the kitten was me. I thought of how easy it would be for me to hurt or even kill the kitten if I was cruel like Arthur and NotDad and then I thought of how brave the kitten was to bite me but not really brave cos it didn't know only that it *had* to bite whatever was holding it and I liked that very much. The other kittens didn't bite but *this* one did even tho it was the smallest cos it had been *chosen* to be the one that bit. Everything in the air in the High Parts around had picked it out to be The One That Had To Bite and I liked that very much and I liked the kitten very much and I decided then and there that I was going to choose it too so I did and put my mark on it but only in my mind and the kitten's bitey mind too.

I put it back into the straw hole and it stopped biting me and I looked at the tiny tiny dinges in my thumbskin made by its tiny tiny teeth and I hoped they would never go. I wiped the tiny poos off my hand on the straw then I stroked Charlesworth again and told her she had the Best Babies Ever and she went 'prrr prrr' and went back to her counter and I asked her for a loaf of bread and a jar of bramble jam and she looked at me and then I heard Arrn bark and go woof and saw him at the bottom of the strawbale hill with his tail going mad and no rat in his mouth unless he'd eaten it cos I'd seen him do that before and it made me feel sick. A *lot* sick. Then I saw Drunkle behind him coming across the yard which was why Arrn was shouting and all hot cos of Drunkle and something was happening. Drunkle had a tent rolled up which he threw into the back of his truck then a rucksack with pans and things hanging from it going clink and then a gun which he didn't *throw* into the truck oh no he lay it down in there all gentle like he put me on the bed from Bala Lake last night, all gentle and kindly but not for the same Whyness as he was kind with that gun. I climbed down the straw hill and patted Arrn to calm him and then went over to Drunkle.

—Bore da, bach. Up early.

I gave a nod to Drunkle and looked at him. His eyes were all in a redness but not like Arrn's ears and there was a kind of blackness around them too, in the skin. His face was like raw mince behind the sprouty hairs and he looked a bit sick but he usually did look like that in the morning-times cos he's my Drunkle and that sick-looking-ness would go away after a bit, I knew that. Same with the smell that was coming out of him like sweat and drink and sick I knew that would go away too after a bit. Funny man my Drunkle looking ill then well again then ill again then well again as if he couldn't make up his mind which way to look or even feel.

—Better go get yurself ready, he said then coughed and spat into the mud and what he spat out looked like one of them mussels in a vinegary jar he sometimes gave me to eat and Keep Me Quiet in pubs. Eat them with little pointy sticks all salty and tastey of the seaside with a taste that went up my nose. I *liked* them mussels in a vinegary jar and the cockles too but I didn't like what came out of Drunkle. — Get a quick shower, put some warm clothes on. Get wrapped up.

—It's summertime, Uncle.

—Not where we're going, bach. Winter all year round up there.

I took Arrn back into the house and had a shower while he went and fetched his beef-bone from upstairs and brought it into the bathroom and lay in the doorway crunching it and licking it and the shower didn't work properly. The water came out only in spurtings like my wee does sometimes when I have to push and it was like the shower was the house's wee and the whole house was pushing it out. And it wasn't very hot which was also like my wee and I thought about drinking it to see if it tasted like my wee but I didn't dare cos it was all brownish and looked bad but it was all just a wee-ey shower and I didn't like it very much and the towel I used the only one I could find was damp and dirtied and smelled like shoes left out in the rain. I complained about it to Arrn but he just went on at his bone but his red ears did go up a little bit so I knew he heard me. Paint was coming off the bathroom walls like the skin of a snake painted yellow and up one wall behind the bath it was going all black like wet dust climbing and behind the toilet I saw stuff growing like crisps stuck into the wall on their ends so they were sticking out like little wavy platforms or like smaller types of that flat platey fungussy stuff that grows on the trunks of trees and I thought of how it was never like this when Auntie Scantie was alive cos she used to Keep Everything Clean and it sadded me a bit cos it made me think of the aloneness in Drunkle growing in him like the stuff behind the toilet since she died. And the blackness in him growing through him like the black wet dust behind the bath since he had to take her down out of the tree With His Own Hands.

The towel didn't take the wetness off me very well at all and even made me smellier than before I'd got in the flippin shower which was a bad bastard business cos it meant that my showertime had been wasted and I hate that wasting of time but nothing could be done cos I can only turn the time back when I'm in My Times and I wasn't then and didn't want to be in them either so I just got on with it and brushed my teeth and put my clothes back on and shivered for a bit and found one of Drunkle's old fleeces in the room by the Bala Lake screen hanging over a chair and I put it on and it made me warmer but it smelled of oil and drink but I didn't really care about them smells. Then I went back outside with Arrn and got a bedazzlement in my eyes cos of the sun on top of the mountain like a crown very bright. Drunkle was leaning against his truck and smoking and staring at that gleamy mountain top with his eyes gone all squinty.

—I'm ready, Uncle, I said.

—Good boy, he said but didn't stop looking up at the high bright sun which reminded me of the fried eggs he made for my tea the day before which made me feel hungry cos I'd only had some milk and an apple so I asked Drunkle if we were going to eat something and he said we'd eat at the pub and flicked his cigarette into the high bright sun and got in the truck so I did too and Arrn jumped in as well, in the back. I saw the leftoverness of his beef-bone in the mud as we drove out of the farmyard but I didn't tell Drunkle to stop for it or anything cos I was tired of Arrn taking it everywhere with him and crunching it and licking it all the time and ignoring me, bloody crunch crunch on it all the time he was. I wound my window down a bit for the good smells to come in and take over the smells that were coming out of my driving Drunkle and thank the Lord they did. Them good good smells in these High Parts.

I asked Drunkle where we were going and he said the Mountain Tavern which gladded me cos it wasn't the Farmer's Arms, the face-scrapey place where I never wanted to go again but did lots of times in the nights in my bad dreams. That Arthur. Creep creep back into the lake and be with your other slimesome chums with big bad teeth like pikes'. We drove even further up into the High Places on to a road with nothing on each side of it but big big space all blue and green beneath like giant waves going out at each side in big big ripples to the sides of the world at each side. I could see each side where the earthball bent cos we were so high and it made me dizzy to think of what we were on.

—I want you to be very careful, Drunkle said. —Don't, whatever you do, let Arrn run mad. Arthur's in a rage about losing another sheep and he needs something to blame it on and if he can blame it on your dog then he will. Won't listen to sense, that man. Told him, I did, I said it's some idiot's exotic pet, either escaped or they've let it go when it got too big and strong and scary for them to keep. Lynx or something. But he's got in his head that it's someone's dog and he just won't let it go. You know what he's like. I told him that dogs don't climb trees but . . .

He shook his head. That was the second time he'd said them words or words like them to me but he'd forgotten cos he's my Drunkle.

—Just keep Arrn under control, anyway. I know he hates being on a lead like but try and keep him on it anyway when Arthur's around. Don't give him an excuse, understand?

He looked sideways at me and I nodded but I didn't really. Understand, I mean. Give Arthur an excuse to do what? I didn't understand so I reached back behind me and stroked Arrn on the head which is what I usually do when I don't understand things and Arrn gave a little happy noise and I heard his tail go whap-whapwhapwhap against the seat.

Drunkle turned down off the Dead High Road on to what was just a High Road. I missed the world from the Dead High Road cos then I couldn't see it all even tho it scared me a bit. We drove into a little village that had a sleeping cat on a car in it and then we drove out of it again.

—What gets me tho is this. Drunkle slowed down so a sheep could get out of his way. He waved it across the road as if it could understand but maybe it could. —Is Arthur's still got his flock. He's one of the few round yur that didn't lose it. Know why? Cos the inspectors didn't visit his farm. That make any sense to you, bach?

Drunkle's questions again which I don't know if he wants me to answer or not but this time I didn't have the chance to answer anyway. I gave him a nod but he wasn't looking at me anyway just the High Road we were on.

—The MAFF inspectors didn't visit his farm so his animals were safe from the disease. See, when they came up to mine and Fay's, they'd just been on an infected place in the bottom of the valley and didn't clean themselves up properly so they passed the germ on to our sheep. Or that's what they *said*, anyway. I mean, there were no signs of sickness in the animals that *I* could see, Fay neither. Precautions, they said. We're gunner have to shoot every last one of these animals as a precautionary measure. And it was *their* fucking fault for not disinfecting themselves in the *first* bastard place. What about *that* precautionary measure, eh?

He shook his head and I could see that he was burning hot and I was getting a bit that way too, in the part where my heart was. The High Places were going past outside the truck behind the window and to me the Inspector-Men with their guns and their Not-Doing-Things-Properly-ness shouldn't've ever come up here because these are not places for People Like Them because everything that happens up here happens because it must and has to and it's always been like that and not as a stupid Precautionary Measure. Things get killed up here because other things have to kill them to eat them and not as a stupid Precautionary Measure. I thought of them coming up here in their white spacesuity things with their guns and all because they didn't clean themselves properly and I thought of me and Arrn and Drunkle, our little Army Of Three chasing them off the High Places and them all running and going 'arrgh arrgh' as they fell off back to the Low Places and didn't kill the sheep as a Precaution Thing and we'd all go back to the house laughing and cheering all three of us and Auntie Fay would laugh and cheer as well and make us all a big pot of cawl to eat cos she'd still be alive.

—So, if you ask me, Arthur should thank his lucky stars that he's still *got* a flock. So he loses the odd one, Christ, we *all* do. Or did. The hawks take them as lambs, or the foxes, or the badgers, or the stoats. The crows, even. What does he expect? He's still got a flock, at least. Still got a livelihood. *And* a wife. Should be on his knees thanking God instead of organising this wild fucking goose chase.

No, Drunkle, I wanted to say, no wild geese would ever kill and eat a sheep. They eat grass, them fellers, not sheep. But I didn't say it cos I didn't think that that was really what Drunkle meant altho I didn't know what he *did* mean and he drove us into another village, a bigger one this time with a school and a shop and everything. I wanted to ask Drunkle if we could stop at the shop so I could get something to eat but I didn't do that either but then I did and he said we'd gone too far past it and that I'd get something to eat at the pub anyway cos Arthur's missis who ran the shop was making breakfast for everyone and I remembered Arthur's missis that time in the shop with her arm in a sling and I thought of her at that moment like I'd never thought of her before and I got hot like I did not when I thought of the Precautionary Measure Men but like I did when I thought of sitting on the horse with Auntie Fay pressed against my back and her arms around me holding the reins cos of a sudden it seemed to me then that Arthur's missis was a bit like Auntie Fay in shapeness cos they were shaped the same. They made the same shape in the air. And I felt funny then cos I'd never thought of Arthur's wife In That Way before nor his daughter too but I started to think of her Like That as well and I got hotter and thought that I might have to hide a part of myself like most men did around Auntie Scantie and that made me think oh no and I got hotter but then Drunkle drove us into the car park of the Mynydd Tafarn and I saw a load of trucks and men like a small army and a couple of bright yellow policemen there as well and that made my hotness go away dead fast and I thought phew and was happy'd.

We parked the truck at the end of the little car park in a space by the stream and we got out and I went to open the back door to let Arrn out too but Drunkle said to leave him there For The Time Being so I waved to him through the window and he looked at me sadded so I waved to him again and told him in my head not to be sadded or worried and he answered me okay which I also heard only in my head but still there was a worryment in his eyes. I followed Drunkle across the car park through the cars and I saw some boys from my school only they weren't from my school any more cos I didn't have a school any more and they gave me looks which made me glad I didn't have a school any more. Their Dads were standing around talking and some of them were checking guns and some of them were drinking tea from mugs and some of them were drinking beer from big glasses or whisky from smaller glasses and they were talking and laughing as if this was all some kind of happy day out and some bright yellow policemen were moving through the crowd talking to the men who had guns and they were trying to be serious and without laughing but I could tell that all this was happying them too. I saw some dogs around as well some of them not even on leads and I wanted to ask Drunkle if I could let Arrn out but I couldn't find him so I looked around at all the people and then I saw him talking to Arthur and half the size of Arthur he was and I remembered then what he said about Arthur and Arrn so I didn't ask him. I smelled something nice and saw some steam in the air in a little cloud above the pub and noticed that people were sipping stuff out of paper mugs that looked like soup cos they had their hands both wrapped around the paper mugs which is what you do when it's cold or early and you drink soup or other hot things out of paper cups so I went over to a place undeneath the floating steam-cloud and saw a table with a great big pot on it and a woman with a scarfness around her head dipping a big spoon in the pot and filling people's held-out cups so I took a cup from the tower on the table and held it out and lovely thicksome soup went in it and well look how much *you've* grown said the scarf-headed lady with the spoon who was Arthur's missis and I went so fast as hot as the soup.

—Haven't *you* filled out, she said in a smile and I hid my face behind my paper cup and didn't know what she meant.

—Last time I saw you you were *this* high, she said and held her hand not far below my chin. I felt heat off her fingers on my face and I saw her fingernails in my eyes quite close and the veins in her skin and the rings on her fingers and the things she wore around her wrist which made a jangly sound. I was making a sound like them too all jingle-jangle but only inside.

—Sorry to hear about Fay, she said in a lower voice. She had been friends with my Auntie Scantie but not Best Ones I didn't think. —How's he holding up, your uncle? Is he okay? Must be terrible for him.

I didn't know what to say so I just told her he was sad.

—Well, yes, I can imagine . . .

I didn't know what to say so I told her I was staying with him for the summer.

—Oh yes? she said and I didn't know if I was supposed to answer but I couldn't say anything anyway cos her eyes got a kind of light in them then and made their drawing-inny darkness not so dark but even more drawing-inny and I *did* think of some words to say but they kind of stuck in my throat like chewy bits of meat so I swallowed the words, with soup, back into the place that made them. Nice soup, it was. It had turnips in it and onions which I like. And the Hot Place in me I thought I might have to hide which made me think Oh No again and sadded me a bit but I was scared too cos Arthur's missis and her eyes and her hands and her Looking At Me and her smile was making me feel things I didn't know what to do with, was making me feel growing in parts and shrinking in others and hot in parts and cold in others and I didn't know what to do so I just drank more soup and remembered of a sudden that her name was Rhiannon and then I noticed too that she had some dark marks on her neck going a bit fadey but still kind of a blueness as if someone had grabbed her there hard. And as *if* I didn't know who that Someone was.

—Well, I'll have to come across and visit you, won't I? she said still with that smiley funny-eyed-ness that I liked very much and was a bit scared of too. — Check up on you both, like. Bring you over some soup or something.

—I'd like that, Rhiannon, I heard a funny voice say. It was deeper and had more out-of-itself-ness than my voice but it must've been me speaking cos I felt the words in my heart area and in my neck as well. This also scared me a bit but then I was nudged from behind and a hand held a paper mug in front of me and it was empty and Rhiannon Smiled At Me Again.

—There we are then, she said and spooned soup into the held-out mug and I took my mug away from her with my hotness and coldness and bigness and smallness and my head went spinning almost like My Times were coming on me but it was different than that it was more to do with things I could feel with my hands or taste with my tongue or smell with my nose or feel pressing against my skin altho it was as big as My Times and filled with things in the same way and I didn't know what to do with this new fast spinniness inside of me. It was fast like a hare or a diving falcon too fast nearly for me to chase or even see. But then one of the boys from My Gone School banged into me and soup spilled on to the back of my hand and burned a bit but not too bad cos it had gone cool a bit but I still looked badness at that boy and he curled his lip up at me like a fern leaf and then went away. I didn't like him and I wished him bad and he did the same to me and I thought of that black hissy mist creeping around him and him disappearing in it and I felt gladder.

I thought of the dance I did when I left the school and was it only yesterday Duw it seemed like ages and I wanted to do That Dance again. I hated that bastard school. Glad dead glad that it was gone I was and still am.

In a sudden the sun went. In a sudden I was in a shadow. I looked up and up and up and saw a big black shape like a bull on its hind legs and knew then that it was That Arthur. A coldness came in me then and I felt dead dead small like a mouse in front of Charlesworth.

—Having a nice chat with my wife, were we? His voice was like a tree falling over into other trees and making them fall too. —Well well. You're going with your pisshead uncle. He'll tell you what to do. And I'll tell you this.

His face was then in mine and much bigger than mine like a mountain itself with the beard like a red forest and cheeks like boulders and his eyes were two Bala Lakes and Duw I could see some monsters in *them* oh yes. I felt mud come into my knees and a coldness come quick into that place that had been hot when his wife Rhiannon put a smile on me.

—Yewer dog goes anywhere near my fucking sheep and I'll blow its fucking head off. Hear me? I'm watching *you*. And your fucking hound. Hear me?

Another one of them questions that I didn't know if I should answer but then the sun was back bright in my eyes cos That Arthur had gone away. Just took all his bigness and *there*-ness somewhere else and let the sun back into my face and I was gladded he was gone cos I hated him being in my eyes and I hated him just for being him and I thought of his wife coming across the mountain in the future-ness ahead to bring me soup and that thought and the thought of the way she looked at me made me glad and less scared of That Arthur and I didn't know why it just did. And Arrn would bite his head off. Arrn would leap and go SNAP and Arthur's stupid too-big head would go off and bounce all the way down the mountain into the Low Places and we'd watch it go and we'd laugh. I'd laugh and Arrn would wag and then we'd go back to Drunkle's house where Rhiannon would be making soup and that would let me laugh some more.

It would be good this world with no Arthur-ness in it. And that's how it should be cos Arthur's not from here anyway and doesn't belong here with me and Arrn and Drunkle and even My Mam Bethan sometimes and he should go back to the place he came from which isn't This World but might be somewhere *in* This World in a lake say or a cave but not here on the mountain that wears the sun. Not here where he can go about his face-scrapey business he should be in the ground with the worms and grubs that bastard Arthur whose wife Rhiannon smiled at me in a way she didn't smile at any other and I didn't know what that meant but did know it made me less scared of Arthur even with his bigness and the badness in me that he made grow.

People started to go off in groups. I saw lots of dogs and some guns. I heard lots of voices with a lot of laughing in those voices and the voices were big and high but they didn't need to be. It was as if most of the people were not being themselves and were speaking loud on purpose so other people could hear them who they weren't even talking at and I wondered why that should be.

I heard a whistle and looked round and saw Drunkle

45

by the truck waving me over to him so I went over to him. I could see Arrn's face behind the back window with his eyes all big and home to worryment.

—Arthur have a word with you, aye?

Yes I said. And his missis Rhiannon did give me a smile that made me hot but I didn't tell that bit to Drunkle.

—I thought he would. You're okay, tho, yeh?

Again I said yes and told him I wasn't scared even tho I was but Rhiannon's smile was still in me.

—Well, just be careful, that's all. I'll keep my eye on that bastard as well but I can't *always* be around, y'know?

He gave me the tent rolled up in its bag and I put it on my back with my arms through the loops and it wasn't heavy at all even tho it would be my home for a bit. I felt like a snail. Drunkle put the rucksack with the clanking pans on his back which went clank and then he put a bottle in each of his coat pockets which made a sort of clanky sound as well and then he put his gun over his shoulder and told me to let Arrn out of the truck and I asked him if I should put Arrn on his lead and Drunkle looked around the car park with no people in it any more and said no it'd be okay but that I should take it with me Just In Case.

I let Arrn out and he went mad, going jump and wag. Drunkle told him to Behave Himself in a voice that had a hardness in it and he stopped jumping and sat and didn't look sad just kind of in a calmness and happy'd to be out and his face with all that in it made me laugh. Drunkle leaned against the truck and lit a cigarette and the smoke went up and then drifted away like a running cloud.

—We're going over the ridge, he said, and made his cigarette point to a High Bit that I could see below the sun. —No, fuck that, we're going *around* the ridge. Take a bit longer like but as long as we get to the stones by night. That's the main thing.

Stones? There were a million stones on the mountain. The mountain itself was a giant stone. —What stones, Uncle?

—Them standing stones. By the spring. I've taken you there before, remember? Twlc y Filiast?

I remembered then and put a smile into the air cos I liked that name and Arrn wagged his tail a bit cos he liked that name as well cos it was *his* name in a way and he understood that and I understood him. Drunkle liked that place, Them Stones, and he had taken me there five times and Auntie Scantie went with us two times as well and I thought that going there again would make Drunkle sad and that made me wonder and I was going to ask Drunkle why we were going there but he rubbed my head which I liked and asked if I was ready and then went off and me and Arrn followed him. Them Questions again. Why is it that grown-up people always ask questions that they don't care if you answer or not? They put a question at you and then just walk away or just carry on talking and I don't know why they do that it puts a puzzlement in me and a wonderment and not like that wonderment the birds put in me or the mountains put in me it is a wonderment that makes me a bit not-nice-hot. Even Drunkle does it but he's my Drunkle.

We walked out of the car park our little Army Of Three and through the village and down a lane and around an old house with nobody in it and over a bridge and over a fence and over a boggy bit that went squish. Arrn loved it, he did, snuffling and sniffing everything he could see and getting all dirty. He sniffed some reeds a bit far away from me and a whitey bird not small flew up screaming and started to swoop on him and Drunkle said it was a harrier probably with chicks and would most likely blind Arrn so he shouted him over and Arrn came with a worryment in his face which made me laugh and the not-small screaming swooping bird went back into the reeds. I liked that bird very much. I'd seen the type of him before but never up that close and I wondered if birds like that had babies like Charlesworth did not kittens of course but if one of their babies would be different to the others, a different colour and a different size and a different Way in it to the others in the nest with him. I hoped they did. I hoped everything did that in the world had babies, not millions of babies like frogs or fish but just a few like hedgehogs or foxes and that looked like their Mams and Dads when they came out of their Mams but maybe a bit different to them like a different size or shape or colour. I hoped all the babies in the world had a chance to be like that, I did, had a chance to come out of their Mams and be borned into the world like that, that's what I hoped, yes.

The ground got more wet and squishsome so we crossed it me and Drunkle by jumping from Dry Hump to Dry Hump but Arrn just ran straight through it and got all mucksome. One big jump at last after loads of Dry Hump Jumps landed us on a path made by sheep and it was drier and better but Arrn didn't seem to think so cos there weren't as many sniffs for him to get all wag-happy'd about. That path took us up to a High Bit and made Drunkle breathe like the Devil's Bridge train whuffwhuff, whuffwhuff and put a harderness in my breathing too and made Arrn's tongue flop out the side of his mouth like raw meat and Drunkle sat down against a rock and I did too and Drunkle began to drink or carried on to drink cos he'd already started back at the pub and he gave me an apple to eat and Arrn a biscuit and I ate the lovely apple and a wind came up from this High Place and pulled my hair and slapped my face it was a NotDad wind and I hated it and wanted it gone. I heard high screamings and looked up and saw big big birds tiny high up in the sky and they made me feel better because I knew I could send them to claw out NotDad's eyes if I wanted to but I didn't want to cos I was better than him but I knew they would if I asked them to.

The High Places are quiet like nowhere else is. They're quiet even tho they're noisy with the windsounds and the high screamings of the high birds but still they are dead dead quiet. Across the boggy bit and over the village on the mountainside far away I could see tiny people moving sideways across the slopeyness of the mountain. Tiny tiny tiny from this very farawayness like the high screaming birds. I pointed to them and Dunkle made his eyes go all thin and squinty then nodded.

—Daft bastards. They'll find bugger all. Beast be fucked. Daft as us, eh?

I asked him if he thought we'd find the thing that was killing all the sheep and he shook his head.

—No.

—Why?

—Cos it doesn't even exist. It's not there.

—But you said . . .

I didn't remember what he said properly but I did remember thinking of lions and tigers roaring cos of his words and Drunkle said that he'd spoke about an escaped Exotic Pet or something *but* and when he said that '*but*' I thought uh-oh cos I knew his speaking was going to go all funny again and he hadn't even drunk very much. And he started then to make words about monsters and demons that are Made By Us and by the energies in our heads, they were the words he used. He said that once we were prey and not predators and that one time long long ago we were the rabbits and not the raptors and that our souls still remember that and keep the monsters at loose in the world and I didn't know what to think or say about that so I asked him why again and he said:

—Cos if you repress a god, you get a demon. Try to fight a destructive power and you do nothing but nourish your own. We *need* monsters to remind us of who we are and our place in the world, to bolt the windows and doors against when it's dark, to define ourselves by what we are not. And if the need to do that becomes so powerful, if we *let* it become so powerful, then . . .

He held his arms out and the bottle went slosh and he made a smile but not like Rhiannon did.

—Mutilated sheep in trees. Because you give it a *shape*, don't you? The darkness, like. You allow it to take a form. We *want* to find sheep torn up in trees cos then we can take up our guns and play Hunt the Monster and do what we think we should be doing, what we think we were put on earth to do. What we *think* our lives should be all about. Doing this makes us feel important, a *part* of all this. We can no more stop ourselves from doing this than we can stop ourselves from going to the toilet when we need to. See what I mean?

He nodded at something and I made my eyes follow his nodding and they saw Arrn in the long grass doing a poo. Just his head sticking up over the long grass but I knew what he doing cos of his face.

—It's all like just a big film, Drunkle carried on saying. —We all have assigned roles and we accept them eagerly only we're too stupid to realise what they are and even if we did we wouldn't care cos we need all this to feel alive. Need to be able to step outside our dull and daily lives and do things that make us feel important, that make our lives worth living. It's like the MAFF men; in a way I can't blame them cos they were just acting against the germ which had been turned into a monster and, really, that's exactly what we're all doing today out here on these mountains. Monsters don't have to be the size of lions to be able to mutilate sheep. Sometimes the monsters are so small you can't even see them. And names; what does it matter what they're called? Can't say MAFF men any more, they're DEFRA men now. But they're still the same thing;

still the fuckers that shot our sheep. Still the fuckers that made Fay . . .

Arrn jumped out of the long grass then and came over to me going wag and I patted him and he jumped away to sniff some more things and he seemed all happy now that the poo was out of him.

Drunkle said: —Grief, for instance. Take grief.

Uh-oh, I thought. A great big UH-OH is what I thought right then.

—Most evil, most horrific monster of all and mainly because it's *there*. We didn't invent it. It's there in the world and you can touch it and see it and we make things up to deal with it and mask it and turn it into something else but we'll always fail because it's too big and we're too weak. We need certain things to make us happy and one of those things is other people but other people die. Grief is the price we pay for love. I saw Fay's face with no life in it and saw the colour she'd gone and felt the weight of her after the life had left her and the space she has left in the world now has been filled only with my sadness. Cos I mean she's fucking *gone*; if I could search every last cupful of space in the universe there would be absolutely nothing of her that I could see with these eyes or feel with these fingers.

He waggled the fingers of the hand that didn't have the bottle in it and drank from the bottle as he waggled them. I didn't really know what he was speaking only that his words were putting a big sad in me and that I wanted to see Auntie Scantie again and hear her laughing.

—See, her death means that there is no *now*. I mean,

I can't look at the clock any more and wonder where she is because she just *isn't*. All there is for me is a past to look back on and at night sometimes I shout out for her to come back, come back to me even tho I *know* she can't. And what she is now, if she is anything at all, is completely unimaginable to me. She is like God. And in the only life I *can* imagine, here on this soil . . .

He patted the mountain he was sitting on like I pat Arrn's head only harder and it made a noise twice.

—. . . God hurts us more than we can bear. More than our worst fears, more than we could ever, ever imagine.

The bottle went glug glug and splish as he drank and his throatlump went up and down twice.

—So let God forgive God. Because *I* fucking can't.

Drunkle's words sent me strange then. He made more words, something about me being Special like he says to me quite a lot cos he's my Drunkle but I wasn't really listening to him I was looking at the grass and feeling myself small on the side of the mountain and wasn't even looking out for Arrn. I was thinking about there being no future-times in front of me no times when Rhiannon would bring me soup or no times when My Mam Bethan and NotDad would Go Their Separate Ways and no times even when I would have My Times or even go back to Drunkle's house and eat fried eggs for my tea or breakfast like little suns. Not all sad this because there would be no times when I would be older and no time when Arrn would die even tho I knew Arrn would never die really in a way cos he'd just leave this earth and go back to the place he came from which maybe all of us do, even Auntie Fay and that's where she is now. But Drunkle said there was no *now* which meant that there would be no ending to anything which meant that everything would die again and again and again too many times to count, they would die every time a tree is blown over and starts to rot away and the platey fungussy stuff like that behind Drunkle's toilet begins to grow and every time someone dies for the first or the millionth time it would be like every other time for everybody else which means that people will be sadded for millions of times more than they would be happy'd which means that the monster that Drunkle spoke about would always be the winner cos nothing would ever become something else.

There was a Sad on me the size of the mountain. There was a Sick on me the size of the world.

We were walking again, me and Arrn and Drunkle, around the ridge of the mountain and we were all without words even Arrn wasn't making His Words inside my head except for Drunkle who asked me lots of times if I was okay and I'd just tell him that I was but I wasn't and I picked up a twig and put it in my pocket and I found a big brown feather from a buzzard and put that in my hair. I found a small bone and put that in my pocket too and another bone with some teeth still on it and I stuck that in the loop of my jeans that the belt goes through and I found another feather black and white so from a magpie then and I put that in my hair as well with the buzzard one and all this stuff the bones and twigs and feathers made me feel a bit better as did the bits of moss and stones

I picked up off the mountain and put in my pockets as well. Drunkle also picked up a bit of stone when we were on top of the ridge and it was dead windy up there and we stopped with the windness around us and he showed the stone to me and it was like a dice with a sharpy edge like we play that game Monopoly with sometimes at night-time in winter only it had a sharpy edge. Drunkle said:

—It's a microlith, see? Long time ago, very long ago, men used these little stones as tools to make larger tools with. They'd get these wee stones and sharpen them on other stones cos the little stones are made from flint or chert, which is dead easy to sharpen. Then they'd use them to sharpen other, bigger stones to make weapons or bigger tools. See?

He rolled the little sharpy dice on his palm under my eyes then he put it in my pocket and I felt it go all warm against me and I could hear it start to make a kind of purrsome noise like Charlesworth does when she's happy or a hummy noise like Drunkle's computer does just before it brings Bala Lake into the room and I liked it doing that.

—Your great-great-great-great-great-great-*great*-grandfather might have touched that very stone. Amazing, innit, eh?

I could tell Drunkle was trying to happy me and I *was* made a bit better by that little sharp-edge dice and by the thinking of my great-loads-of-times taid touching it and it lying there for ages on this mounain and me coming along and picking it up or no *Drunkle* picking it up and I was a bit happy'd because it told me that there *is* a future-ness and times-to-come

55

because there I was with the little sharpy stone, wasn't I? So there *was* a future-ness which meant that things *could* get happier no matter how much of the sadness or the sickness was on you and in you. And I felt the little toolstone in my pocket going glowy and going *mmmm* or *prrrr* and oh on the mountain I felt things moving through me deep in me moving like the brown river on the other side of the village all that way below, moving yes through me like that brown river the gravy Teifi or like all the things broken down to mush ages old and sunken in its gravy waves. Like them like *it* like them *in* it they moved in *me* or *it* moved in me.

I felt my head go funny. All kind of floppy and wobblesome like mud and I felt worried.

—Uncle . . .

The mountain flopped from side to side. Bad taste sicky feeling in my mouth.

—Uncle . . .

—What, bach? What's happening?

Drunkle held my moving head in his hands and I could see his face all big and close but not like Arthur's I *liked* Drunkle's face being big and close it made me better and it wasn't like Arthur's, no.

—What, bach? Tell me what's wrong. Are you going away? Are you having a Time?

I shook my head cos I didn't think I was but I wasn't sure only that everything had gone flopsome on the mountain and in me. Arrn was looking up at me all worried with his red ears down and a mucky face and Drunkle was still holding my face.

—Deep breaths now . . . breathe deeply now . . . relax, bach, it'll pass . . .

Innnnn. Ouuutt. In. Out. Wind on my head and passing over it like the mountain breathing like me the wind on my head was the mountain's breath. Innnnn. Ouuuutt.

—Aw fer Christ sakes . . . your mother should've given me some pills. Jeez that bloody sister of mine . . . bloody useless she is . . .

—It's okay, I said to make his face push at the worry I could see in it. I didn't like seeing Drunkle's face like that nor Arrn's either so I told him it was okay too but only in my head but the worryment stayed in both their faces so I told them again it was okay both with my tongue and in my head which I could do cos my tongue had then stopped tapping in my mouth and the bad sick taste had gone away and my head had then stopped wobbling in the mountain's breath.

—You sure?

I didn't want to nod cos that would make my head feel wobblesome again so I just gave him a yes.

—Think you can make it down the hill? The stones are there. The spring is there.

No nod just a yes.

—I'll put the tent up and you can have a sleep.

No nod just a yes.

—You can make it, aye? It's not far. Want me to carry you on my back?

No shake just a no.

—I'll carry the tent, then.

Drunkle took the tent off my back and made me not a snail any more and he put it over his shoulder and then he had the clanky sack on his back and the tent over one shoulder and the gun over his other shoulder and bottles in his pockets too and it looked too much but he still held my hand and took me down off the ridge and along the dry path made by the sheep and Arrn stayed by my side too and I was happy like that with Drunkle and Arrn and holding Drunkle's hand even tho I wasn't little any more I was sixteen years old and a man My Mam Bethan would say and NotDad would say those words too but in a different way. And we all three in Our Little Army went down off the mountain into the bottom of the valley where it went all squishsome again so we walked around that bit and around a big hole in the ground a big dark square hole where an old mine tunnel had fallen in and there was no bottom to that hole and we went around a small hill and I heard water laughing and then saw that water coming out of the ground in a little spring and it better'd me very much cos the squishsome bit was bad and the spring wasn't, everyone knows that. And there were two big stones standing up out of the ground and taller than Drunkle more tall even than Arthur and I sat down with my back against one and ate some biscuits with Arrn and Drunkle put the tent up on a dry flat bit of ground and unpacked the stove and got some water from the spring and boiled it and made tea and I drank a cup of tea out of a cup made of metal which burned my lips a bit and all the time Drunkle was asking me if I was okay and it started to rain a bit even tho it was summertime and Drunkle told me in a nice and not a NotDad way to go into the tent for shelter and I did and I felt happy in that tent with Arrn with the

soft rain outside and very soon I fell asleep. I liked
them stones, named after Arrn. I liked that spring with
the laughing water. I liked being in the tent with Arrn
lying by me and Drunkle outside with his gun against
the monsters and I liked Rhiannon bringing me soup
in the futureness and I liked being in the High Places
miles away from NotDad in the Town in the belowness and all of them things were why I fell asleep so
very soon and easy.

I was waked up by a drummy noise, the noise of
the rain on the tent sounding like a drum. The noise
was in my head too between my ears and my hand
went out for Arrn but he wasn't there so I sat up and
moved on my bum to the door of the tent which
hadn't been zipped up so it was open and I looked
out at the watery world, the mist and the mountains
and rain falling down all over everything and I saw
Drunkle sitting up against one of them two tall stones
and he was wearing an orange anorak thing with the
hood pulled up and he was drinking from a bottle cos
he's my Drunkle and Arrn was with him too and Arrn
saw me then there in the tent-door and he came over
to me doing a wag and I patted his head and he came
inside the tent with me and sat by my side. Drunkle
saw me and smiled.

—Feeling better, bach? Bit of sleep sorted you out,
aye?

I didn't know the answer to that cos I'd only just
waked up so I just drank some water from a bottle
instead and asked Drunkle if he'd seen any monsters
or beasts while I'd been asleep.

—Not out *here*, boy, no, he said. He kind of waved

his bottle at the mountain and he said the word 'here' as if it weighed more than his other words. —There's some food in a bag there for you. See in the pocket?

He pointed to the side of the tent and I saw a bulge in that-sided-ness and I reached over Arrn and took out the bulge and it was a white Co-op bag with some food in it, a Mars bar and a pastie and an apple and some crisps. I opened the pastie and Arrn's red ears and his eyebrows too went up at the rustlement so I gave him a bit of the crust and he ate it and I ate as well.

Pat pat pat went the rain. Pat pat pat on the tent.

I asked Drunkle if he wanted to come in the tent with me and Arrn out of the rain but he said no he was okay. Said he liked the feeling of the rain on him and that the stone he was leaning against was all the shelter he would ever need altho I could not see how that could be cos I mean what if it was to go all of a sudden stormy? No roof on the stone it just went up and didn't stick out or anything nor did the other one next to it. They were both just two tall sticky-up stones like an eleven.

Drunkle was going to start speaking His Words, I could tell. Was going to start telling his stories like he does but they're not really proper stories I don't know what to call them I just call them Drunkle's Words.

—See that? he said, making a point with his bottle hand into and through the rain which pat-pat-patted on the tent. —See that mound over there?

There were millions of mounds out there and I didn't know which one he meant so I just told him yes. Arrn nose-nudged me so I gave him the last bit of pastic and I started to eat the Mars bar. I mean the whole High Places were moundy. A million massive mounds there are in these High Parts.

—It's called a tumulus. It's a burial mound. Some people call it a barrow but barrow, tumulus, it means the same thing. Inside it there are the bones of a person who was very very important to the people that used to live up here. There'll be bones in there, and trinkets, things like jewellery and weapons and other bones too maybe of that important person's dog or horse. Dogs were revered by those people, see. Cos of their role in hunting.

I put one hand on Arrn's back the hand without the Mars bar and I felt his back go up and then down again in a softness as he breathed because he was alive and not just dead bones in the mountain and I was glad dead glad of that.

—Might even be the bones of the animals that were hunted, deer or something, boar, cos them people killed things not in the way we do today, no, they killed them to eat and wear and make things out of from their bones and sinews and hooves and stuff. Antlers and teeth. They saw it not as conquering other animals but more of an, an *acceptance* of a bounty from the prey species. Or the prey spirits. The *spirit* of that species. Understand me? Or does it sound like I'm talking shite to you?

One of them questions again and Drunkle not even looking at me as he asked it and oh Drunkle you are talking shite to me and pat pat pat went the rain the voice of the rain one of the sky's hundred voices and no question in that at all or ever just pat pat pat pat

pat. I looked out at the mounds from my dryness, looked out at the wet mounds from my chocolatey and doggy dryment and I saw them mounds as graves and thought of the bones in there for so long deep in the mud and stone and thought again that yes there *could* be a future-ness. And as I thought of that the future-ness and the past-ness when them bones *weren't* bones but had skin and meat on them and were living walking things started to move towards each other and uh-oh I thought cos it might be bad if they met. If All Times came together it might get bad and turn into My Times.

Wobbly head? Yes a bit. Badsicky taste? Yes a bit but hard to tell behind the Mars bar. But the beaty voice of the rain on the tent and some flashing in the sky over the Highest Part which could just be some lightning but no thunder I could hear. And the Times coming together uh-oh FLASH behind the mountain top it came and went again.

I touched my head to feel the feathers in my hair and felt them there and was gladded they hadn't fallen out while I was down in sleep. Felt the bits of moss and stone and stuff in my pockets and beltloops and stuff and was better'd a bit by them.

Pat pat pat pat pat.

—See, these people, they put their stamp on the landscape, on the entire country. Christ how they did that. Every lump in the ground can be significant, every bulge or hillock can have a meaning. These people, they drained lakes, burned vegetation, felled forests, enclosed huge areas of land with walls and banks and ditches and changed the pattern of the landscape and so changed the pattern of history. Tombs and barrows. Tumuli and standing stones put up a thousand years before the pyramids and for what purpose, eh? Aligned to face east, most of them are, face the rising sun and for why?

Drunkle looked at me this time as if he wanted me to give an answer but I couldn't and not only cos of the chocolate and not only cos of the bad taste behind it and not only cos of the wobbling and not even cos of the Times moving to meet each other across the tops of the High Parts where the flashing was going on. Not cos of any of this, no.

—Vast applications of willpower and muscle-power to construct these things, see. And why the connections with the stars or the calendars? Why the correspondence to the equinoxes? Eh? Know anyone who can answer that?

Oh Drunkle I thought please stop these questions please they are making my head wobble more.

—Sun and moon and their movements all magical. We've found sheep bones drilled with small holes into flutes. Ancient fucking music, boy.

Music like the rain like the sky's drum drum. Been there for ever this music even when dinosaurs were in these High Parts and maybe there's still one of them Up Here and that's what's killing the sheep. A dinosaur over *there* and a spaceship over *there* and they're moving towards each other to meet.

Pat pat pat. Pat Arrn on the head. Pat the wet tall stone you sit back against like Drunkle did and it makes a wet slappy noise kind of three times.

—The enormity of the task, to erect these stones

up here. To cut them from the rock down below and drag them up here and all for what purpose? For reasons never to be known, to only be guessed at somewhere between signposts and objects of calendral, calicrend, *calendrical* reverence and you know what the odd thing is? What the real puzzle is?

No Drunkle no but I did not say the word.

—It's that *we* put these stones up, me and you, and we haven't got the first fucking clue now why we ever bothered. We have the same blood still in us, or some of it anyway, as the people who put these things up and we've forgotten everything we ever learned in those times. We don't have the first bastard clue any more, do we? No, we don't. Cairns, for instance; what do they *mean*? Placed on summits or ridges so everyone could see them but what the fuck for? Ashes have been found in cairns, bones as well, and beakers. Cups, like, y'know? And in these cups they've found evidence of intoxicants. Cannabis even.

Drunkle grinned big and waved his sloshy bottle at the High Parts around again. I saw him grin and the whiteness of his teeth inside the orangeness-made shadow around his head.

—Intoxication, bach, eh? So many kinds of that. See, over in England, when Christianity came, they linked these stones with the Devil.

Three times slap again pat pat pat.

—Here, tho, they're linked with people. We link them with *people*, see? With *us*. With me and you. With your Mam and with Fay and with fucking Arthur even. With everyone. And they make my fucking head spin, boy, they make me drunk, like, and d'you wanner know why? Cos they tell us of mankind's perception of itself; they show us how we have viewed ourselves at different stages in our evolution. So, see, in the Middle Ages these stones were put up by magic and a race of ancient giants, but now we see them as Stone Age computers, like the one at my house that shows you Llyn Tegid. We've always said that some of these stones spin or dance or swim, often at important times of the year. We say that, if removed, they will return. We say that they can grow.

Not dinosaurs or spaceships but wizards and computers then moving towards each other. Moving towards each other across these High Parts and when they meet oh when they meet. Stones going spinny like my head and doing a dance like I did when I left the school everything moving together all Times together and oh when they. What will happen when they.

Drum drum went the rain.

—We talk about a race of giants who hurled rocks about as pebbles. Druidic altars or worship stones! Sacrifice stones at which dreadful wails can be heard! Pain and sadness! Pain and sadness! Witches' covens meet within these circles, we say. And did you know, at a place called Y Meini Hirion in 1958, they exhumed skeletons of cremated children, both eleven years old. Eleven! Pain and sadness, boy!

Oh Drunkle please do not shout please bring your voice down again so that it does not bounce off these High Parts and them rocks like an eleven. Eleven eleven. All Times All Things they come together and them rocks like an eleven go right up to the sky.

—And why? What were they doing there? Petrified criminals, these stones could be! Bad people turned to rock by the hardness of their hearts! Dolmens built to hide the treasure of the Teg, the Tylwyth Teg! Shapeshifters! Descendants of pre-Christian gods! Entities driven out by Wesley's men because to them the Teg were from Hell! They lured young people into dancing and drinking. Aw Jesus, got to stamp that out. And Christ the Teg had their own language! Didn't speak English! Can't have that, no, stamp it out! Talk like us!

Rain's speaking drumming drumming one of the speakings of the sky. A speaking of the falling water on the tent pat pat and a speaking of Arrn's breathing and it All Coming Together all Times meeting *on* me and *in* me turning into one Just One.

—Da yw'r maen gyda'r Efengyl, Drunkle said and in my head I said oh Drunkle please stop these words of yours. —Good as the stone together with the gospel, bach, eh? Good as the oh Jesus Christ what's wrong are you okay?

Drum drum drum. All Times meeting coming together everything *in* me everything *on* me just One Time and it is Mine it is

My Times.

—Oh God, bach . . . oh bloody hell . . .

I felt Drunkle lift me and I saw bright lights flash then FLASH in my brain nowhere else not behind the mountain top nowehere else but In My Brain. I heard the laughing water I heard the laughing in the springing water and Drunkle put me down by that laughing water and I could feel the rain pat pat on my face and I saw the sky all grey even tho it was summer and then my eyes went rolling and I could see Arrn he was with me and I could see crows flying they were with me too and then my eyes went rolling some more and I could see the inside of my head where the FLASH was happening that FLASH that FLASH and I could also see

The world go away. The world go so small like a pea blue and green so far so far away. I could see crows holding me up, holding up my arms and legs and they flapped and lifted me up into the blackness into the highness the very-far-away-ness so the town and the High Parts and the planet they stood on turned into just a pea blue and green so very far away all in a belowness to me. Drunkle was somewhere on that pea. My Mam Bethan and NotDad and Arthur and Rhiannon and everyone was somewhere on that pea so was Arrn oh God uh-oh Arrn was so very far away from me. And everything that had ever happened on that pea and *was* happening and would *ever* happen on that tiny pea blue and green floating in all that blackness and space was *on* me and *in* me and I knew everything about it everything everything oh yes I did. And of a sudden the crows all went, they flew away and I fell a bit but then was lifted again by just one bird this time a hawk his claws in my back holding me up with no pain and I could see his beating wings on each side of me and see his face above mine and he took me even further away from the floating pea and out of the blackness around me and into a kind of bright white light where he let me go and flew away like the crows did but I didn't fall I just kind of lay in the brightness as if it was a pillow all around me and I saw shapes and I heard noises and Everything was in that light. Snowball the bull was there and Bethan before she met that sod NotDad and Auntie Fay too came out of that light all with a smiling on her and she wasn't in a tree and she didn't have a rope around her neck she was just putting a smiling on me and kind of all around me she was cos I mean she had her arms around me from behind like when I would go on the horse with her but I could see her in front of me as well cos of her smiling like she always used to put at me cos she liked me did my Auntie Fay before she became a branch on a tree and I liked her as well. And in that light she told me she was sorry that she'd made hearts break but that she wasn't sorry for what she did cos there were things Down There that had to stop and she then told me that yes there *are* and *will be* future-times and that I would be better'd when I went back Down There and that Drunkle must be better'd too and she laughed then cos I didn't know she knew about My Word Drunkle and I didn't ask a question but she heard it anyway and told me there in that light that she now knew Everything, all that was gone and all to come and she said that we will have Bad Times but that we will Come Through them and I didn't know what she meant by that and I asked her in my head what she meant but her arms then went away from me and I wanted them back around me but she shook her head and then the shape of her was kind of swallowed by a much bigger shape which wasn't really a shape cos it was Everything All Around. Yes it was a kind of all-around-ness which was Everything. It was the names of every raindrop that had ever fallen on to the earth and It was everything that had ever happened EVER from when the earth was born til when it would die, every blade of grass and the dying of every fly and even of the smaller fellers that live on them flies yes even them and every war that turned people into them flies cos they're only as important as them when they get splatted like them too and every egg ever laid by spider or by bird and every whale and every wave and every grain of sand on every beach and everything everything which made me feel funny as if I would get one of My Times in one of My Times and I didn't like that thinking even tho I would've just Let It Happen if it was going to happen and the Everything shape kind of sucked me into it kind of even closer to its centreness and then so quickly and of a sudden I felt sadder than I had ever felt before. Sadder even than when Dad left or NotDad hit Bethan or when I got duffed up at the school sadder than when Snowball died or even Auntie Fay. I didn't know that there could ever be that much Sadness and the Everything Shape told me in a headvoice that was my *own* voice that the world now a pea so far away but so so big when I was on it was made of that Sadness and I thought of how big everything was when I was on that world which made me think of how big that Sadness was and I started to cry then cos it meant that everything Down There was sadded even Arrn and there was nothing any of us could do to stop it and just then when I started to cry and needed the Everything Shape to put its arms around me and better me like Auntie

Fay did a little bit It turned away. The Everything Shape saw me and heard me crying and then It turned away as if It wasn't bothered and It knew that I needed It to do what Auntie Fay once did but It didn't care and It just turned away which was strange cos It was Everywhere and Everything but still that's what It did It looked away from me when I needed It and it was like going to Drunkle for help and him just laughing at me or Arrn biting me and I hated It for turning away and I was going to shout at It but then of a sudden it was like I kind of fell through It, fell through the cushiony cloudy thing and whooshed fast through the blackness past the pea and then underneath the pea and no Good Hawk to hold me this time I just fell into a scary blackness like Bala Lake where there was no light and the blackness was like a cold sliminess pressing up on to my skin and face and I hated it very much. It didn't hurt when I landed in it but I did still hate it cos of the coldness and the sticksome blackness and then I could kind of see into it like when the Leccy Runs Out at My Mam Bethan's house cos NotDad's Drunk The Meter Money and I have to sit in the darkness until it stops being dark, that's what it was like there in that sticky black Belowplace it was like I could kind of see in the blackness and it was like I was in a great big cave and I could see things that I didn't really want to see I saw a man so thin I could see his bones and he had teeth bigger than his head and he told me in My Own Voice that he was the Lord Of Want and then I saw a very big fat man with arms where his legs should be and legs where his arms should be and he said that

70

he was the Lord Of Misrule and then a man with a
small swarm of wasps instead of a face and he said he
was the Lord Of Disease and then a shape came to
me with a heart the size of a car sticking out of his
chest on an arm like a squid's arm all suckery and he
said he was the Lord Of Longing and he stood there
in front of me and that giant heart made a squishsome sound and kind of folded open and it smelled
like Drunkle's farmyard after Fay became a branch and
I saw in that heart all the things that made that sadness
that I felt Up Above in the brightness and there was
millions of them sad things that flew out and around
me all fizzy like a cloud of things so small that I
couldn't even see what they were, just dots like the
eyes of maggots but millions and millions of them and
they shaped themselves into four claws in front of me
like a big big buzzard's foot and each claw grabbed
one of my arms and legs and then before I knew it
my arms and legs were off and the swarmy claws were
holding them up in front of my face and it didn't hurt
and at first I was kind of interested in seeing my own
arms and legs off like that but then it was like they
died and that sadded me again cos it was like bits of
me were dead then and I hated it. And then my arms
and legs flew around my head as if I was a planet and
they were moons doing an orbit-y thing and them
Lord fellers laughed and one told me that I was looking
at the Fundamental Information Of Human Existence,
they were the words he said, and the information was
aloneness and danger and the badness in the world
around everyone that will always want to smash any
happiness and I asked them Lordshapes if they were

ghosts and they laughed and said that they were Just
Like Me and then they went away and then a skeleton
came in front of me and I knew that that skeleton
was me, my bones there like the ones under the mound
that Drunkle spoke his words about way up there on
the pea up above me now and I wasn't scared looking
at myself as a skeleton in fact I was better'd by it a
bit even without my arms and legs cos seeing me as
a skeleton was like seeing myself set free from something as if let out of a cage and seeing them bits of
me that will last the longest against the monsters and
even the sun and wind and rain. It was like something
heavy fell off me as I looked at my boney self and
not just my skin and meat I felt kind of lighter and
was happy'd and I laughed even and when I laughed
the swarmy claws put my arms and legs back on the
skeleton and then picked me up and put me on the
skeleton too and it was like I was a New Person with
new eyes then cos then I could see up into the floating
bluegreen pea and see the Everything-ness in that pea
and how sick and ill and dying it was and as I looked
at that I felt something like an arrow in my chest and
that hurt loads but not cos of the arrow, no, it hurt
more cos of all the people I knew then were dying
and in a sufferment on that pea which I knew then
wasn't really small like a pea it was massive like something I can't say what because nothing is as big as it
or ever will be. And I looked into it and knew what
I had to do what a Massive Job I had to do I had to
look away from everything that had been and gone
so I could make a New World which is really what
My Times are but I knew then that I had to do it for

the whole world and not just for me. And the Lords started to drift back at me in a Not Friendly way like Arthur in the pub car park and I started to get scared but then I heard a scream and the Good Hawk swooped and the Lord fellers ran away in fearment and I held my arms up for the Hawk like a baby does for its Mam and the bird picked me up and I was safe and it took me up til the pea turned big again and I closed my eyes cos of the whooshy wind in them and when I opened them again I was floating over the High Parts and I could see loads from up there, I could see the hole in the ground where the mine shaft had fallen in and I could see the ridge and the tent and the stones and the spring and I could see Drunkle holding another person in his arms and Arrn was running around Drunkle all worried and then I saw that Drunkle was holding *me* and I wanted then to go back into my body so the Good Hawk let me go and I fell, I fell into the stream and I was waiting for coldness and a shockness but there was none of that cos I was a fish as soon as I hit the water. I felt my fins and my tail and I liked that and I knew the place where I'd been borned loads of miles away but I knew that if I wanted to I could swim all the way back to that place, jumping up waterfalls and swimming up streams and all great stuff like that and I liked swimming in that stream then with the other fish and the weeds and the newts and a crayfish looking out at me from underneath a mossy stone and I saw a hole in the bank so I swam into it and zoomed along through a thin black tunnel and uh-oh I thought I am back in the Lordy place but no cos I then shot out into white light like a bullet from a gun, shot out in a stream of water into the air dead close to Drunkle and My Body and when I landed I landed in that My Body and I could then of a sudden feel wetness and a shakingness and Drunkle's arms heavy around me holding me and I could taste a bloodment in my mouth and I could hear Arrn whining and I couldn't move. I had my arms and legs back on me again but I couldn't flippin move them. Couldn't talk even. Couldn't do anything sept open my eyes.

—Oh thank Christ thank Christ . . . you've come back to me . . . oh good Jesus . . .

I felt Drunkle's bristles all a-prickle on my face as he kissed my head. I looked at Arrn and he stopped his worried whining noises and went wag but he still looked dead worried. I wanted to pat him on the head but I couldn't move my arm.

My Times.

My Times.

Drunkle looked into my face and I saw the redness in his eyes but not like Arrn's ears and the red veiny spiderwebs across his nose and his chin-bristles like a crop. He asked me if I was okay and I could nod then so I did and he took me into the tent and put me down in a gentleness and he pulled the sleeping bag up over me and told me to get some more rest and Arrn came into the tent too and lay down by me and I lifted one arm and put it down across him and he liked that cos he went wag and Drunkle smiled too but both of them still looked dead worried and I thought of the illness that waits for them and the sadness in and under everything but I didn't tell them about them things and I thought I knew what I had to do but I wasn't sure.

Sleeping, it's like My Times. Cos falling asleep or falling into My Times it's like I'm nothing but in the seconds before I fall into them I am happier than I have ever been before in my life. Even with all the things I knew then about the Lords and the sadness and Everything else, all them things I knew and didn't know what to do about or with I was very much happy'd to be there with Arrn and Drunkle, in the tent in the wet High Parts, falling into sleep in my head, oh yes.

My Times this is what they are like. Sometimes they are like this.

It was still dark when I woke up and I knew I was still in the tent cos I could feel the side of it pressing against my face a bit cold which I didn't like so I rolled over on to my back. The sleeping bag went tighter around my body. I couldn't hear the rain go pat pat on the tent any more so it must've stopped but I could hear two snorings, one from Arrn and one from Drunkle, and I could smell Arrn's dogness and the drink coming out of Drunkle's snorings cos he was my Drunkle. I knew where I was, oh yes, in a tent in the High Parts by a hole in the ground and the spring and the stones, that's where I was, and there was a beast somewhere outside in them High Places but I was safe from it in the tent and warm and dry with the two snorings around me and I felt happy to be there. I liked being in that tent between the two snorings.

I thought about My Times and about the last one I'd had with the sadness and Fay and the Lordy fellers and my arms and legs going off. Always My Times were a bit like that, as much as I can remember them, always the going-up-ness and the pea planet and the birds and the talking with the ghosts and stuff but never before had I seen My Own Bones like that or had my arms and legs going off like that. I'd seen crows and hawks and other animals and things in My Times in fact there are *always* crows in My Times lifting me up off the ground but never before that Good Hawk which came to save me. I'd been a salmon as well before in My Times and a hare as well and one time even a bat but never before had I swam up through a spring like that and back into My Body like that. And I'd never been told of that sadness stuff before and the illness stuff, I'd never been told about them things before but it was like I'd known that stuff all along anyway and the Everything shape and the Lordy fellers just told me things that I knew anyway but I'd never *felt* that sadness before, never had it put in me like that before. And I didn't really know what any of it meant only that there was something I had to do not really with my body and arms and legs outside on the world but kind of *in* me somewhere in the place where the Teifi runs when I'm just about to have a My Time. In *that* place.

Dreams and stuff, the things I see in My Times, they all go away when I wake up or Come Back. They all go fadey like the photographs of *her* Mam that My Mam Bethan keeps on the dresser. They all go fadey, kind of brownish and you stop being able to see the

people in a clear way any more and they go into a
ghostment and that's what it's like when I wake up
from dreams or Come Back from My Times and sometimes I wish it wasn't like that but It Is. They might
mean nothing they're just My Times. Just my dreams.

I'd had them before and I'll have them again I
thought then and started to nod off again in the safe
dark tent with the snorings and the smells and the
beast-world outside. And as I fell into the sleep again
I started to see things, other things in my head even
tho it wasn't a My Time but I saw other people having
Their Own Times, in other countries far away and in
other past-nesses, people like me but *not* like me,
Eskimo fellers in the skins from seals having Their
Times on fields of ice and red-skinned fellers having
Their Times in snowy forests and fellers wearing blan-
kety things in deserts and black fellers in Australia and
Africa and places like that. Some of them were Long
Ago and some of them were in the Present Day and
some were even in the Future-times like Auntie Fay-
in-the-whiteness told me there would be and all these
people were having My Times but they weren't My
Times of course they were Times Of Their Own but
then I knew that I had brothers and sisters all over
the world and always had had and always would have
even tho we would never ever meet and they would
be dreaming of me too and I liked that thinking very
very much.

I was better'd big by that thinking and that dreaming,
that there was people like me All Over The World at
all different times. All of us doing the same thing,
having Our Times in our Own Different Ways and

places. No need to feel so lonely, see? No need to feel so sad. And I fell into the sleeping with a smiling part inside me going glow like a little sun like the fried egg I hoped Drunkle would be making for me in the morning when I woke up.

A mushy blackbits banana and a cup of tea no flippin fried egg.

—Get it down you quick, boy. Packing the tent away soon. How you feeling?

I told Drunkle okay but I wanted a fried egg.

—Up here? And where am I gunner get eggs from up here then? Buzzard's egg for your brekkie, is that it?

He smiled and patted my head like I pat Arrn's and I felt a bit happy'd by that but was still eggless.

—I'll make you all the fried eggs you want back at the house. Hundreds of the buggers.

He went back out of the tent and I opened the banana and it was yick so I gave it to Arrn who ate it cos he'll eat anything then he went fast outside the tent probably to do a poo. I sat up in my sleeping bag and drank the tea which was hot and nice and put some clothes on and felt something sticking in my ear and it was a feather, the sharp end of a feather like people used to write with. Forsooth and prithee. It was black and white so probably a maggie's. It didn't need to be there any more so I took it out of my hair then took out all the stones and bits of moss and stuff from my pockets and dropped them by the spring when I'd got outside the tent then looked at them in the mud there at my feet then pushed them into the water with my shoe-toe and they went plip and sank except for the feathers which floated like little flat boats.

Drunkle was packing stuff away, pans and his gun and stuff. I asked him for some toilet roll and he gave me a roll of it and I climbed a little mound and went down behind a rock and had a poo like Arrn did and wiped my bum which Arrn does sometimes as well on the grass but I used toilet roll and then I put another rock on top of the poo and went back down off the mound and helped Drunkle to pack stuff away. We took the tent down and rolled it up and put it in its sack and I put that on my back and I was made into a snail again or a crab. Drunkle put all of the rubbish into a plastic bag that said LIDL on it and was yellow and blue and then he put that into a bigger bag which he put into his rucksack which he put on to his back and he was snail'd too like me. He put his gun over his shoulder as well and it stuck up over his head like one of them horny eye-pole things a snail has and he whistled Arrn who came and then we all three in Our Little Army went away from the stones and the spring and the big deep hole in the ground back over the ridge and the boggy bit, back towards the pub where Drunkle's truck was waiting.

We didn't say much on that walk back. Drunkle just looked ahead of himself with his hands in his pockets and didn't say many words and didn't drink from a bottle which put a surprise in me because he was my Drunkle. Even Arrn didn't say much, with his tongue-slobbery mouth or in my head, and he didn't do his normal Arrn-y stuff either like run around like a mad thing everywhere sniffing or whining or growling he just trotted towards the pub ahead of us as if he was the Army Leader stopping sometimes to look back at us over his shoulder to check that we weren't lost. And I didn't say much either cos there was enough words going on in my head about the pea planet and the Lords and the sickness and the sadness and all those other things I'd learned in the last My Times. I didn't really feel like *me* any more, not properly, after all that. It was just a My Time which I've had hundreds of before but after I've Come Back from them I've always felt like Me but I didn't then cos it was as if I'd been changed in that last My Time. Still Me but a different Me there were new things I knew but didn't know I knew them and then of a sudden I did cos the Fay-ghost and the Everything-thing and them horrible Lordy fellers had told me them and that made me different but I was still Me underneath it all cos there were things I still didn't know why or how I knew like why I can understand Arrn when he speaks to me sometimes or what a buzzard is saying or what a fox says or why that little black-and-white kitten was chosen to bite Me.

We came down off the Dead High Parts and on to a flat bit between High Places and I didn't remember crossing that bit and was going to ask Drunkle about it but he shook his head and told me to shush but not in a NotDad way and he pointed out into the field and there were loads of things to look at in that field and I didn't know which one of them he was pointing at so I just looked at them all or just at those ones I could see with my person's eyes. There was a fence going across the flat bit with dead crows nailed to the posts like black rags and their wings flapping a bit in the wind as if they were still alive and trying to get free. And there was a tree all twisted and burned and black cos once it had been Struck By Lightning and around the bottom of that tree were lots more crows and they were all kind of hopping up and down and flapping their wings but not taking off and they were making their Crow noise kind of like a laughing and a bark but also not like a laughing or a bark at all.

—They're having a parliament, Drunkle said in a voice all low and whispery and then most of the crows went quiet but they did not look at me or Drunkle or Arrn, they just went a bit quieter and stopped flying and jumping so much and just started walking around the tree looking at the ground with their wings folded and it was like they had their hands behind their backs and were walking and listening and thinking and were all important.

—I have come to tell you that my wife is dead, Drunkle said in a louder voice to the crows who carried on walking around the burned tree and staring at the ground. Some of them pecked at the ground really hard and it was like they were stabbing the mountain with their beaks like blades. —She took her own life by hanging herself from the branch of a tree. I had to take her down myself and I carried her dead body with me for some time. My heart is broken now and will be for ever and to me the world is a lot less without her in it. I am shattered by her death and I will never be the same man again but my heart continues to beat and I have accepted that and I will let it. But I need you to know that there is no longer a Fay in the world. She is dead and gone for ever and nothing will ever bring her back.

The crows marched and pecked as if they were thinking about them words of Drunkle's then Arrn made one woof of a sudden and that made all the birds flap up into the air making a cackley noise but they didn't go up far cos they landed in the branches of the black tree. It was then like they were the leaves of that tree and them also made black, burned too by the lightning. They settled in the branches but carried on making a big noise as if Drunkle's news had given them Something To Talk About and they all now had an excitement on them and in them and it made my head go spin cos they were like talking leaves and one time I'd had a Bad Dream about that and I thought of the crows that had carried me off last night in That My Time and it made me go more spinsome and I looked up at Drunkle and he was giving a bit of a smile to the sky and his skin didn't look as yellow and his eyes didn't look as red and he looked down and saw me looking up then he put his arms around my head and pressed it into his chest and it was warm and nice there and I could smell a saltiness and an oiliness in the clothes on his body and woodsmoke too and I could feel the weight of him against my face not as heavy as normal and then he let me go and I patted Arrn who wagged and we went back to the pub still not saying much but Drunkle seemed better'd somehow, more happy'd, and his feet did not make such a loud sound when he walked across the empty car park when we got back to the pub which Didn't Take Long At All.

Empty of people I mean but full of cars with no people in them. We put the stuff the tent and things into the back of Drunkle's truck and then we got into the truck and we drove away, back to Drunkle's house. All the other people must still have been out in the High Places looking for the sheep-killing thing and I wanted to ask Drunkle why we weren't still out on the High Places too but I didn't cos I liked going home better and when we got back to Drunkle's smelly house Arrn took off across the yard probably to look for rats and not the black-and-white kitten I hoped and me and Drunkle took all the stuff the tent and things back into the house and Drunkle made eggs like little suns with beans as well and toast and tea and we ate it all in the kitchen watching the little telly in the corner and I liked it there in that kitchen with my Drunkle and the food and the sunshine coming in all slanty through the window. No nasty Lords in there, oh no. No Everything-thing turning away altho of course that *was* in there because it was Everything it was in the eggs and the beans and staring up at me out of the tea in my mug and hiding in the oven and even on the telly but I wasn't scared or sadded by that, there, then. After the food I went up to watch Bala Lake and look out for the monster but nothing moved across the lake except for a few small slow boats and the breath of the Everything-thing and I watched that for a bit then felt tired of a sudden so I turned Bala Lake off and got into the bed and I heard Drunkle downstairs whistling and I could smell bleachy stuff coming up through the floor and then I heard a Hoover and Duw Duw I thought my Drunkle is having a clean.

I lay on the bed in the Hoover-ness from below and closed my eyes so I could still see Bala Lake only not on the screen any more just in my head. I liked the lake being in my head all in a peacement and no monster in it and me floating in it and it all warm not cold like I knew it would be in Real Life and no monster in it either again not like Real Life. Just me in my head in the warm floaty-ness. I thought of the screen that let me look at Bala Lake and the webcam that showed me each little ripple on it as it happened in Real Life and me miles away from it but still seeing every ripple and wave and the boats going across it at the same time as they went across it in the Real World and it was like old wizardy fellers with glass balls in the Olden Days. I knew that there were people who understood it all and could tell me if I asked them how such things like that could be but I knew I wouldn't understand their words and so it was Magic to me cos I could never understand how I could see things miles and miles away over all them High Places as them things really happened. It would always be Magic to me, that would, oh yes. That thinking made me feel funny and spinsome, how one person could be looking at Bala Lake standing right by it and seeing the same things that I could see hundreds of miles away and it was as if the world was shrivelling up dead quick like when I put an empty crisp bag on the red coals in the fireplace and spin went my head so I rolled on to my side and put a pillow over my head and tucked my ears in, folded them in against the sides of my head. And I thought then about how lucky we are that we've got bendy ears cos if they were hard like our fingernails we wouldn't be able to tuck them in so we'd have to sleep on our backs or our fronts all the time so our ears wouldn't snap off and if we slept on our backs we'd all snore loads and if we slept on our fronts we'd all probably smothercate and die so hurray I thought for our bendy ears.

I slept for a small bit cos I don't think I slept very well in the tent the night before, not after That My Time, and Arrn woke me up when he sniffled his wet nose against my face and the first thing I saw when I opened my eyes was his red ears going glow. I rolled on to him off the bed and we had a little play-fight then I got a shower in Drunkle's bathroom which was of a sudden all clean with the wet black dust gone from the wall and the platey fungussy stuff gone and even the towel all dry and fresh and smelling of a niceness not like old socks. Amazing, I thought. Drunkle has Cleaned Everything Up. I put new clothes on well not new but clean and put the old ones well not old but dirty in the washing basket and then went downstairs and there was my Drunkle in the kitchen sitting at the table and that kitchen too was all Dead Clean, no dirty dishes everywhere and all the tops and machines and things all in a gleaming. Drunkle put a smile at me.

—What d'you think, bach? Could eat your food in here now, couldn't you?

He waved his arm around the kitchen all pleased and happy'd with himself and what he'd done and I told him it looked dead nice and he put a smiling into the kitchen which made it even nicer and he said he was going to take a shower and that we had to go back to the Mynydd Tafarn so he went upstairs and I went outside. As soon as I opened the door Arrn came crashing down the stairs and ran outside into the world and ran round the yard like a mad bugger, all muck flying out from his feet cos Drunkle hadn't done to the yard what he'd done to the kitchen but that was okay cos cleaning up the yard would be a Big Job. An All Dayer. Maybe even a Two Dayer. I went over to the barn and climbed Straw Hill and saw Charlesworth at her counter and I asked her for a packet of tea and a pound of streaky and she just watched me with her green green eyes which closed all happy'd when I stroked her head and made her go prrrr. I looked into the hole in the straw and saw the kittens all curled up together in a furry bundle sleeping with their tiny sides all going in-and-out slow cos they were alive and they were all asleep even my little black-and-white bitey mate and I wanted to pick him up so that he'd bite me again and feel him in my hand all small but still alive but I didn't cos he was in sleep and I didn't want to wake him up or break his kitten dreams. I watched them for a bit as Charlesworth watched me as well then I went down off Straw Hill and saw Arrn at the doorway to the cowshed looking in with his red red ears all standy and his tail all standy too so I went over to him and stood by him and he put a little growl into the cowshed and I looked into there too and could see nothing growlful but I knew that Arrn was seeing the bull, Snowball the bull who got shot ages ago when he went mad but who still lived in the byre in a way. And as I watched I saw a shadow come out of another shadow and that shadow moved and it was like a tractor it was so big and I heard it make a rumbly, grumbly sound and then I thought that it might bellow and I didn't want to hear that it would be too scary and Arrn growled again and fearment came on me out of that shadow then Drunkle's voice called me and the shadow in a sudden went and me and Arrn ran away back across the mudsome yard and Drunkle was all clean in his truck and we both of us got in as well, me in the front next to Drunkle and Arrn in the back on his own. Arrn was dead mucky and I got some muck on my new clean clothes too but I didn't care cos well I just didn't. Drunkle started the engine of the truck and for a bit it sounded like Snowball's grumble and I didn't tell Drunkle about the ghost bull and I reached over backwards and stroked Arrn and then we were both better'd and Drunkle sang us a song as he drove us back towards the pub.

On the Dead High Road he stopped the truck next to a slopey field with a burned tree in it and some crows around that tree. It might've been the same tree that I'd seen earlier and the crows might've been the same ones that we saw then too and who knew about Fay being dead and Drunkle's heart being broken and so in fact were different birds than before because of that knowing in them now. I didn't know. They looked the same as them and were walking the same as them but that didn't mean anything but Drunkle was looking at them like he looked at the other ones and he turned the engine off and let us hear the wind and the noise of them crows. The wind brought Drunkle's clean smell into my nose and it was not his normal niff of drink and sick and stuff it was all of a soapy-ness and fresh like flowers. But even tho he was smelling different he *wasn't* different cos he started talking His Words again like he always does cos he's my Drunkle.

—Listen to the crows, he said. —What d'you think they're saying?

One of Them Questions again. Always Them Questions of No Answers even if an answer was asked for which it never flippin is.

—Well, whatever you think it is . . . you're wrong.

Flippin cheek I thought cos I *knew* what the crows were saying to each other even if I couldn't've said it in Person's Words. I've known what the crows and in fact *all* the birds say to each other since I was a pram-babby but I've never told any other humanperson about that cos they wouldn't know what I was talking about if I did and anyway it is a Secret between me and the birds.

—See, their calls are not for us, Drunkle said, — only for other crows. They don't care about us. Whether we live or die, as an entire species I mean, is of no importance to them whatsoever. They've colonised the entire planet, these birds, even the poles and the deserts. Only one other species can make a similar claim.

I thought of the crows carrying me up into the Lordy-place and being with me in My Times as they always are and I got a bit smiley somewhere inside. Arrn snuffled the back of my neck with his wet warm nose and I then got even more smiley and wanted to laugh but thought that that wouldn't fit with Drunkle's words and the way he was being right then so I didn't laugh cos that might've put a sad on him.

—Birds of death, we call them. Their blackness and their stalking and their carrion-loving ways. Long ago, they learned to follow armies because of the easy feeding they'd have on the battlefield. Familiars of witches, we say. Gods and goddesses of war. They're so important to us but they're utterly indifferent to us themselves. They seem to be waiting patiently for our era to pass, don't you think? And we put all this stuff on them, we make them into these ill-omened things, yet watch them play; note how they seem to love their lives.

I watched them walk and hop with their wings folded behind their backs like hands and I watched them beak-stab the mountain and watched them fight and play and flap up into the branches of the burned tree and then fly back down to the ground again. Glowing black all the time their feathers so black that their wings did shine as if they had some silverness in their feathers and even their black eyes seemed to go glow as well. Even Arrn was watching them with his tongue out a bit and his eyes kind of in a deepness as if he wanted to be with them as well and not in the car with me and Drunkle.

—See the way they leap and walk? I mean they can fly, but they seem to prefer to strut and jump. Why? Why should that be? We don't need an ornithologist to analyse their behaviour, we need a fucking psychiatrist. They've been observed making tools; they are said to have emotional awareness. We feel a need to deal with them in our lives in some ways but all we've come up with is the name 'crow' which is just a poor attempt to mimic their call. Their voice. Which may be all we have left of magic, as if in naming the bird we summon it with a call. Its *own* call. Its *own* name.

We watched the birds for a bit all three of us and I listened to them speak inside my head. They made words in my head and I made words back to them and I knew what they were doing there on the mountain top, I knew what they were up to cos they told me and anyway I always have. I told them in my head that I would see them again soon and Drunkle put his fingers on the key to start the truck up but as he did that two more black birds came to join the crows, two birds *like* them crows but much bigger and they landed in the middle of the crowness like helicopters or something and started to make barky sounds at the crows which made them fly apart and scatter. Some of them hopped away and some flew up into the tree branches but all of them made their sounds.

—Ah, now, ravens, Drunkle said and let the key go out of his hand. —Unusual to see them among crows like this. They're usually solitary things, living as couples in remote areas like this, even more remote really. I wonder what's brought them among the crows? Cousins of course but different birds. Avoid each other normally.

I knew because them ravens were telling me but I couldn't tell it to Drunkle in his Words cos all I had were Raven Words to tell it and no one else I knew could ever understand so I said nothing with my Tongue but everything with my Head.

—He's a trickster, that raven, Drunkle said in a not-heavy voice as if he didn't want Raven to hear. — He can do everything the culture forbids. Only he can spew death out again. One of those ravens could be a dead king; Bran could be his name, in fact *is* his name in the language of this place. Flew all the way back here from the Tower of London to revisit the land of his birth and death. Both creator deity and agent of destruction, that's him. Both holy and obscene he is. Completely beyond our control. The courts they hold; ever seen them? *I* have; twenty or so birds will surround just one bird and make a lot of noise, building themselves up into a frenzy until they all turn on the one bird and kill it. Savage it into a mess. I've seen them do such things. Several times. We can never understand.

He looked a bit sad then Drunkle did as he looked out of the window at the birds. The ravens flew away and the crows made a crowd again at the bottom of the burned tree and I watched the two ravens as they flapped slow over the mountain top and then off the mountain into the sun and the misty-ness that was starting to happen just beneath that sun. I wanted to stop Drunkle from looking sad but I couldn't tell him about why the crows did what he said they did but I thought he wanted to hear that Why but I couldn't tell him of that Why cos it wasn't in any of his words or mine it was in different words that came from the crows and also as well the burned tree and the grass and the rocks and all the little insects in them rocks and that grass and it was even in the words of the mountain itself. Words not mine and words not

Drunkle's and maybe that was why he was sad and I thought then that maybe this was what the sadness of the world was made of that the Everything-thing told me about cos nearly all of the people on the world only had Their Own Words and could never understand the words of anything else even tho they really really wanted to so it made them dead lonely. Cos they lived in things and in a place that they can never understand all around them everywhere are things they can never understand and that's what has made the big big sadness on the world and put a big big sad on everyone who lives on it and why they are all mad.

—Aw Jesus, would you listen to me, eh? Drunkle put a smile out of him at me. —Talking pure bloody shit I am. Been living alone for too long. Talking this way and I'm not even drunk. Daft.

Then he showed me a big smile and I showed him one back and then he started the engine and as the truck began to speak Arrn woofed behind me all happy and his tail went whap whap on the seat.

—Soon change that tho, bach, eh? Let's go to the pub.

We drove away from the crows and the burned tree and off the Dead High Road and down on to the Just High Road and we started singing 'The Rattling Bog' and got to the pub at the 'bird' bit which is great. We stopped in the car park which was full of cars and we sang the last long bird bit dead loud:

> And on that nest there was a bird
> A rare bird! A rattling bird!
> And the bird on the nest

And the nest on the leaf
And the leaf on a twig
And the twig on a limb
And the limb on a branch
And the branch on a trunk
And the trunk on a tree
And the tree in a hole
And the hole in a bog
And the bog down in the valley-O!
Roll, roll, the rattling bog,
The bog down in the valley-O!
Roll, roll, the rattling bog,
The bog down in the valley-O!

We sang that and got all out-of-breath and laughed and Arrn joined in with some woofs and happy'd we were All Three. I remembered Drunkle first teaching me that song when I was little and we went up the hill at Abergynolwyn and we climbed to the top and looked over at Cader Idris and we saw a load of people on the same hill as us but lower down and they were all singing and I asked Drunkle about their song and he taught me all the words and I like to sing it. I like it when it gets all long at the end and I can't find my breath to finish it and nor can Drunkle and our voices go all kind of stretched out and it makes us laugh. Auntie Fay used to like it too. She used to like singing it with me and I was waiting for Drunkle to get sad again then but he didn't he just put a laughing in the car and put a rubbing on my head and he then got out of the truck and I patted Arrn and told him not to worry, we wouldn't be long and he looked all worried anyway with his ears all red and I closed the door and waved to him and went with Drunkle into the pub.

But those people who I remembered singing, Drunkle knew some of them and I remembered him telling me that some of them were dead and some of them had Gone Away and one of them or maybe someone that they knew had become a murderer and a few years ago killed some people in the hills for No Reason he just went mad and killed them and when they found out his friends, maybe some of the ones who I saw singing, well they killed him too. I remembered Drunkle telling me all that one night when he was drunk and it Stuck In My Head like burrs stick in Arrn's fur but it wasn't News to me about the world or about the things that live on it it was just something more that Stuck In My Head like the ravens' voices do and the foxes' stories and the world with those stories in it could not be bigger than it was in my head but I knew that very much it was, very very much indeed oh yes. People kill and get killed and sing songs together on hillsides and how could that be bigger?

It was people-packed and smokesome inside the pub and loud with all their voices and the song in the grey air behind their voices not loud but it would've been without all them voices on top of it. Some of the people standing by the door turned to look at us as we went in and some of them gave a smile to me and Drunkle and some of them rubbed my head and said 'shwmae bach' and spoke more and other words to Drunkle but some of them did none of those things

they just looked at us once then looked away cos they
were probably friends of Arthur or if not friends of
his then they probably believed his big bad fibs about
Arrn killing the sheep and so they did not like my
Drunkle or me and did not want to speak to us but
I didn't care about them and nor did Drunkle and
nor would Arrn, if he knew. Drunkle went to the bar
side-on like a crab and I followed him walking That
Way too so's I could fit through all the people-
packedness and I felt a big Looking on me but not
like them Eyes I feel on me in the High Places which
are everywhere, no, not like that, this was a big Looking
from all the people squoze into the pub, a big big
Looking from Their Eyes and so I gave a Looking
back at them with my own eyes which I mightn't've
been able to do had I not met them Lordy fellers the
night before and been to That Dark Place above the
pea planet. And it was like I had new and bigger eyes
after that My Time cos I could look back at that big
Looking and see all the people that were making it,
see all the people from roundabout who lived in the
High Places on the hills and mountains, see them with
beards and not with beards and with hats and not with
hats and some of them not with ten fingers or not
with the normal amount of teeth and one or two even
Not With Two Eyes in their faces to do their Looking
with. I saw Bobi Cyclops who one summer was putting
up a fence and the wire he was stretching went twang
and broke and the staple shot out of the post and went
in his eye and he had to go to the hospital like that
For Treatment with the staple sticking out of his eye
as if he was a kind of post himself and that's how

come he could then only do a One-Eyed Looking. And I saw Michael the Mittens who was once at the bottom of a deep hole with a ladder going down into it and he called up for a shovel and the feller up above slid the shovel down the ladder but Michael the Mittens altho he wasn't Mittens then he was just Michael ap Huw was holding on to a rung and the shovel went down and sliced all his fingers off except for his thumb and I saw him there in the pub at the bar, the mitten on one hand hiding his fingerlessness and the fingers of his other non-mittened hand holding a small glass with a bit of brown drink in it. Michael the Mittens gave a smile to me and did a kind of salutey move-ment with his mitten like a soldier and I gave a smile to him back and he moved away a bit so's Drunkle and me could get to the bar and buy some drinks which Drunkle did, a Coke for me and a beer for him cos he's my Drunkle but no whisky to go with the beer and I was surprised at that cos he's my Drunkle.

I didn't like my Coke it was warm and bubble-less. The barman told Drunkle to go in the back room where the pool table was kept.

—Some kind of conference going on. Your pres-ence is requested, I imagine.

I heard Drunkle make a sigh but couldn't see him do it cos of all the packed people and then we went into the back room and I thought great cos we were going to play some games of pool but there was a big board across the table with some food on it, sand-wiches and sausage rolls and stuff, and some people were sitting on that board as well and lots of others were sitting or standing around it and the air in there had gone all fogsome cos of the smokeness which made my two eyes put out water and also made me cough a bit too. It went a bit more quiet when we went into that room me and Drunkle and I felt another Big Looking go on me, still big but smaller than the first one which was smaller than the other one I feel on me when I'm in the High Parts which is bigger than All Lookings ever. I heard Arthur's voice say somewhere in the greyness:

—Oh well Christ look who it is. Nice of you to join us. Gracing us with your presence, is it? Sure you can spare the time? I mean brave man like you, got a flock to protect, haven't you? Stock can come to harm out on them hills.

I heard him laugh and I heard a few other people laugh too but it didn't sound like they meant their laughing, they were just wanting to be like Arthur. I saw Drunkle throwing a Bad Look from his two eyes across the boarded pool table and I followed that Bad Look with *my* two eyes and saw Arthur sitting on two chairs put side by side at the end of the pool table on the other side of the room drinking from one big bottle with one hand and his other hand was on the back of Rhiannon's neck who was sitting next to him. It looked like Arthur was holding the back of her neck quite hard and it looked like Rhiannon didn't want him to do it cos she was looking down at her two hands which were wrapped around a glass held in her lap which meant that I couldn't see her two eyes which meant that she wasn't looking at me which meant that I didn't go burning hot but my belly did go a bit wobblesome when I saw her and my brain did bang a bit at the grippingness of Arthur's hand. Arthur was pouring drink into his beard from his bottle and I wished Arrn was there with me with his ears all firesome red but he wasn't he was alone in the truck outside in the car park and probably going all fretsome and whiney like he does when he's alone and I knew that cos I can hear him even when I'm not with him.

—Not *my* animals getting ripped apart and thrown up trees, Drunkle said and I heard some people make a gaspy kind of sound and saw heads swing to put their Looking on Arthur and I did the same with my head and saw Arthur slowly take the bottle out of his beard and saw Rhiannon look at him side-on like Drunkle and I had to walk to the bar with her two eyes dark and her two eyes big and then I went just a little bit hot.

—No, cos you've got no fucking animals left, have you? Arthur's voice was like a rock falling far away and in a rumbleness getting closer. —Cos the MAFFmen come an shot em all, didn't they? An you were a-cowering in your fucking cowshed. Where, if I remember it right, you'd already lost a bull cos you can't control your beasts. Give us all a bad fucking name, do people like you. Can't even control that hound of yours. Wild fucking goose chase across the mountain and everyone knows it's that fucking dog of yours. Got it outside, have you? Fetch it in here. I'll do the job with a snooker cue, boy.

I wondered what job Arthur was talking about and imagined him playing pool with Arrn, Arrn on his back legs lining up a shot with a cigarette in his mouth at the corner and one eye all squinty with the smoke like I've seen fellers do and that then put me in a puzzlement but then another voice sounded from a feller sitting on the board on the pool table, a feller who I knew a bit cos he was the vet and I'd seen him up at Drunkle's farm a few times to look at the animals when Auntie Fay was still alive and riding on her horse. I liked that feller, that vet; he told me stories about when he was in Africa working with African farmers and I liked them stories. Liked thinking about the elephants and giraffes and hippos and things.

—It's not a dog, Arthur, he said, even tho everybody in that room was listening to him. —I've told you before, mun; it's not a dog. No dog has the muscle to drag a full-grown sheep up a tree and what kind of dog climbs trees anyway? Plus the nature of the wounds, mun; it's a feline of some sort responsible for wounds like that. I saw similar damage in Africa. Want my opinion, you've got a leopard loose out there. Someone's had it as a pet and it's grown too big and they've thought 'oh shit' and let the bastard thing loose out on the mountain. It's not a dog, mun. You're barking up the wrong tree.

Only me and him and Drunkle laughed at his joke and Arthur of a sudden was standing up with his head nearly touching the ceiling-beams and he slammed his bottle down BANG on the pool-table board and people jumped and quickly I looked at Rhiannon and saw her face looking like Arrn's does when I leave him alone all in a worryment and then I quick-looked up at Drunkle's face and I could see his teeth and a jumping thing in his cheek and his eyes with sparks in them. Lots of eye stuff going on tonight, I thought. Lots of stuff happening in people's eyes as if nobody could speak to each other out of their mouths only their eyes or if they did speak with their mouths then they were telling lies and it was only out of their eyes either one of them only or both if they had two that their proper meanings were coming.

—Well, let's see then, shall we? Arthur's voice was like a bull's. —I'll go and snap that fucking dog's neck and let's see if I or anybody else loses any more stock, eh? Leopard be fucked. It's that bastard dog and I know it is.

He came towards me through the people like a bull on its back legs and people moved apart for him and I looked up at his head way up there in the rafters and his beard all like a fire and he was like a mountain moving towards me and then in a sudden his face was below mine all in a looking-up-ness cos I heard Arrn woof in my head and things went FLASH like lightning in my brains like Fay's ghost and the Everything-thing and the sadness and the danger of the whole world and I knew what to do and so I jumped up on to the pool table to be in a bigger-ness than Arthur and that's how come he was looking up at me and I wasn't scared in fact I was so very burning hot and his face was down there not as big as usual and I felt my hand go up with the Coke glass in it to hold it above both our heads and the little biting kitten was in me and Arrn was in me and the buzzards were in me and Auntie Fay as in me and the Everything-thing was *in* me and *on* me and I raised that glass above my head and above Arthur's head too and I felt the mountain I was on turn and move in *me*.

And I would've put that glass down hard on Arthur's head like he put his bottle down BANG on the board, I would've, I was going to whack whack whack that bastard Arthur on top of his stupid head with my glass of horrible no-bubbles drink but I got of a sudden a big distractment with my head all the way up there in the rafters cos it was a place I'd never been before, way up there in the beamy ceilingness, and I could smell years and years of cigarette smoke coming out of it and it was horrible and I saw a web right by my two eyes with no spider in it but some dead flies in it and one still alive kicking its legs and going buzz with its wings and I started to think then about how lucky spiders are cos they live in their own chip shops, they don't have to go out and find their food cos their food comes to their houses like knock knock who's at the door oh it's a beefburger or knock knock who is it it's chips with peas and gravy oh thank you. And that thinking made me forget why I'd jumped up on to the pool table and it must've been only a second but it seemed like ages and I went into a long spider-ness in my head and I could see everything with my eight eyes cos that's how many eyes spiders have and they must be able to see Everything with their eight eyes. Lucky spider fellers to be able to see all around them and live in their own chip shops and then in a sudden I realised where I was again and I looked down and saw all the starey faces and saw Arthur's face fiery red looking up at me and saw his arm swing out behind my knees all that way below and he pulled my knees quick into his chest and I went backwards very very quick and heard a THUNK and felt that THUNK too in my head like a bomb going off a bad big noise inside my brainbits which made Everything go black.

I must've slept for a bit then cos of the dream I had, a dream of playing pool with my head as the ball, little so's it could fit into the pockets. And I must've had a normal head on me as well cos I could see my own other head little on the table all worried and I was playing pool with Arthur which wasn't Right cos I'd never have a Happiness with him in it and I went to break the balls and my second head the little one was going no no and screaming and Arthur was looking at me and going grin all big.

When I came out of that dream I was in Drunkle's truck on the back seat and Arrn was standing across me and looking down at my face like he was going to lick it. I pushed him away a bit cos I don't like him licking my face with the tongue he licks his own bum with but I was happy'd to see him. My head was hurting, the back bit of my head was going ache and had a soreness and I rubbed it and felt a lump. Arrn made a whiney noise and leaned back against the door looking at me all worried. Bastard Arthur. Bite him Arrn, bite his stupid fiery face off and drag him up into a tree and leave him up there to bastard die. I felt another face then in the truck with me with eyes that were putting a Looking on me but not as hard as the Looking that had happened in the pub and I saw Drunkle in the front seat twisted round in his body so he could see me. He was putting a smile on me and he reached over to touch my face and I felt the skin of his fingers all rough and raspy against the skin of my face.

—You okay, bach?

I nodded and my head went hurt in that nodness. Which meant that no I wasn't *really* okay but I didn't want my Drunkle to know that.

—Good boy. You're a good boy, you are.

His smile grew a bit and he stopped touching my face then and I wanted him to carry on cos it made my head not so sore and achey.

—Everyone's cheering you in there, y'know. He nodded the back of his not-sore head at the pub. — Or we would be if Arthur wasn't raging like a fucking lunatic. But they're all saying how brave you are and how proud of you I should be. And I am. You know that, don't you? How proud of you I am?

One of Them Questions again. Always Them Questions that people ask and don't want an answer to. Usually asked by grown-up people as well and why do they do that? Always asking Them Questions and not wanting you to answer them cos they answer them themselves:

—Yes, I'm sure you do. So, so proud I am. Wish you were my son. The son I couldn't have with Fay.

No because you can't have a son with someone who's dead. I wanted to tell Drunkle about Fay and how happy she was now in That Place up above the pea planet but I didn't know how to say it so I just asked him when we were going to go home and he said very soon but that he had to go and help Calm

Arthur Down first and he asked me again if I'd be okay and again I nodded yes and made my head go a-hurting again and Drunkle said he wouldn't be long and left the truck and went back into the pub and then I was alone with Arrn again which is most times How I Like It. Just me and my dog Arrn together and the world outside the truck and that's just how I like it best, oh yes.

I sat up on the seat and put my arms around Arrn and he made a kind of whuffle noise with his flop-some lips and lay down across my knees. I felt him all heavy on me and felt his back all strong and felt his heart beat slow against my legs and looked at his ears in their redness in the lightment from the moon. I stroked him and looked out of the window and saw that moon made lots of times over in the windows of the parked cars and trucks and tractors and I looked at the pub all lit up and I could hear a noisiness from in there which was quiet to me but I knew it was loud to the people in there cos I could still hear it even through the bricks and windows and moony dark air. The engine of Drunkle's truck went tick. Tick. Tick without any tocks and I felt Arrn all warm in his body across my legs and I stroked the back of his neck and I looked out of the truck at the world outside it which at that moment was all just in the shape of a pub and maybe the mountain behind it too which I knew was there all big in the blackness even tho I couldn't see it cos of the nightness all around. And I saw a shape run fast across the car park out of some trees and into some other trees and I knew it was a hare, a long-eared long-legged feller very fast going like dark low lightning across the car park between the cars dead quick shadowflash then gone. I liked that very much and I was happy'd loads to see that hare. That hare my friend. That hare from the moon from that Everything-thing how less we would all be on this spinning pea planet without you.

I saw the door to the pub go open and light and noise came out in a short gush and my heart jumped up a bit in me in case it was Arthur and for a moment I felt it go bang behind my eyes but then it settled back down in me again cos quickly I saw that the person was much too small to be Arthur. But then just as quick it came jumping up again cos I saw by the hair and the shape and the moving that it was Rhiannon and hot I went like soup and just as flop-some inside. Just as hot and flopsome as the soup she handed out yesterday morning nice soup it was with turnips in it with her wrists all bangley and lights in her dark eyes like sun on frosty grass when it goes spear-spikey and white. Nice soup before That My Time before I was me then when I was different.

She looked around the car park with her head going to the left then the right and then she put her head straight on and saw the truck with me in it and came over to it moving out from the lights of the pub into a darkness then into a lightness again this time from the moon and she waved at me by making her fingers on one hand go waggle and she smiled at me through the window of the truck and I saw her teeth white in the nightness and I started to go hotter and hotter and when she opened the door of the truck and got into the front seat with her smells and hair and bangleness I went so hot that I was burning. Felt like lightning had struck me like it had struck Crow Tree and all's I could do was look at her and smell her and she sat there in a big Smiling with half of her in a shadowment and the other half lit up in a bluement from the moon. I looked at her and swallowed but nothing went down into my bellyness where the fire was.

—Your head okay? Caught a hell of a whack you did.

I told her in a voice that didn't sound like mine that my head was fine and Arrn raised his head off my legs to put a Looking at her but he didn't go growl or say his name and Rhiannon reached between the seats with her bangley hand and scratched Arrn behind one of his redsome ears and he closed his eyes and took his Looking back into himself and he let her scratch him for a bit then dropped his head back down on my legs again and Rhiannon took her hand back.

—You did a great thing in there, she said and I didn't know what she meant. Not great to slam your head WHACK on a pool table and go into a sleeping. —Arthur didn't have a clue what to do. Made him look a right twat, you did. Wonderful it was.

Her hand came back between the seats then and I felt it close to my face and I thought I might blow up like a bomb and not a balloon if that hand were to put itself on my face but when it did I didn't I just went even hotter and even more soupsome but it wasn't a hotness that burned like a coal from the fire it was like a hotness that wanted to make all the world good and me in it. Rhiannon only touched my face for one tiny moment and then she took her hand back again but I still felt it on my face even when it wasn't any more.

—I've got to go back in, she said. —He'll be looking for me. Gets suspicious if I'm out of his sight for ten bastard seconds. But I'll come and see you tomorrow, bring you over some cawl or something. Brave tough boy like you needs feeding up if he's going to take on the world, aye?

Bigger went her smiling and her eyes more drawy-inny and of a sudden I felt a place on my belly go lovely and warm, just one spot of skin on my belly go all glow-y and nice like a fire in the snow like it was the best place in the world and I realised then that Rhiannon had just touched me on that place. Just kind of poked me all gentle with her finger and now of a sudden that tiny spot on my belly where she touched was marking me out as the Most Important Person in the whole world and I wondered what would happen if she touched me There again.

—Tomorrow then, she said and got out of the truck and an emptiness came into it very very quickly. She turned back to waggle her fingers at me again and I saw her walk across the car park and I saw her move and I saw the shape she made in the moonlight and the dark air around her and I felt my face glow where she touched it and I also felt my belly glow where she touched it and then I felt the back of my head go back into a throbment and I wondered how that could be, how the touch of two people on me Rhiannon and Arthur could feel so very different. And

I wondered as well why people lived with each other if they hated each other like Rhiannon hated Arthur and he hated her and why people don't just go away from each other if they don't like each other and can't stand each other or why they even thought that living together would be a good thing in the first place and I asked Arrn but he didn't know and anyway he was all asleep and didn't hear me.

I lay back on the seat with Arrn like a blanket on me. Bits of me went glow and made a nice hummy noise like a bee on a flower and one bit of me banged and hurt and made a noise like when you switch the telly on and there's no picture only a cracklement. I felt the High Places all around me outside the truck and I thought of Fay and the Everything-thing and the Lordy people all looking down on it all and seeing all the things on this planet that people do to each other, the puzzlement of it all, and I wondered if they had the Why of it all and if they'd tell me when My Times come again. And I thought of My Mam Bethan and NotDad and if she would ever be happy again and I hoped she would but didn't think that that would ever be so.

Drunkle got back in the truck quite soon after Rhiannon got out but I was more than half in a sleeping by then. Sleep was on me more than halfway. And I thought of Rhiannon then Arthur then Rhiannon again and then again Rhiannon and then nobody else but her and I felt through my sleeping the truck begin to move and I couldn't smell the drink in Drunkle which was strange cos he was my Drunkle and I wondered about that as I went properly into a sleepment and even in that nice nothingness bits of my body still glowed and stayed warm, oh yes.

I dreamed that night that I lived under the ground in a burrow like a rabbit or a badger or a fox and it was dead nice down in that burrow it was snug in that burrow and warm and I was safe in my soilment. I curled up all cosy and I could see daylight shining from Way Up Above but it wasn't really *that* far and I lived *in* the mountain in my dream not *on* it. And I heard a voice calling my name and I went all floaty up towards that bit of daylight and I went into and through it and carried on floating up *off* the mountain and up and further up into the daylight of the brightsome bluesome sky where there was no clouds only That Voice calling me and I thought that it might've been Fay's voice but I never found out cos when I looked down and saw the mountain all small way way below me and no crows or hawks or birds of any sort to hold up my arms and legs and keep me from falling I got all scared and started to fall and that's when I woke up so it was the kind of dream that I don't know what to do with but maybe I'm not supposed to do anything with it anyway.

But it seems I dreamed a lot, last summer. Every time I fell into the sleepiness a dream would come and get me.

When I woke up I saw Bala Lake on the screen on the desk by the window but no monster, no. I couldn't see Arrn so I got out of the bed and went in my nudiness over to Bala Lake and saw a note from my Drunkle telling me that he'd gone into The Town to get some things to clean up the yard with and I was surprised at that cos he's my Drunkle. I looked out of the window at the mucky yard and saw Arrn down there and when he saw me he wagged and went woof and I told him in my head that I'd get ready and go down to see him and he ran off behind the cowshed again probably to chase rats like he liked to do. I didn't mind him chasing rats cos that's what happy'd him and That's What Dogs Do but I didn't like it when he caught them and crunched them and killed them cos the rats were just being rats and not needing painfulness or murdering but Arrn is a dog and That's What Dogs Do even tho his dogness is different to other dogs'.

I watched Bala Lake for a few minutes but no monster came so I went and had a shower in the new clean bathroom and cleaned myself with soap and amazement cos the bathroom was so clean. Couldn't flippin believe it. I felt cleaner when I got out of the shower than when I did get in which was the first time I'd ever felt that in Drunkle's house since Fay went and then I put some clothes on and went downstairs into the kitchen which was all clean as well and I made some toast and ate it with jam on then drank some milk and then took an apple outside into the lovely brightsome day which stayed bright even down there in the dirtment of the yard. The sky was all blue like it had been painted that colour and I couldn't see any clouds in it only a burning hot sun like them bits on me that went glow when Rhiannon touched them yesterday only much much bigger and far far away of course but still the same and I pointed my face towards that sun and closed my eyes and let it dry me and clean me again too with its heat even tho I was already clean cos of the shower and the new clean bathroom. I liked the feeling of the sun's smiling on my face and I smiled back at it then I went across the yard and up Straw Hill and Charlesworth came out to see me and went 'mew'. Half-dozen eggs and a pound of butter please. I stroked her with one hand and ate my apple with the other and my teeth of course down to the sharpy pippy centre bit then chucked it away off the hill and it sank into a mud pool with a squelchy sound. I looked into the hole in the straw and saw the kittens all asleep except for the little black-and-white feller so I reached in and picked him up and it was again like I was picking up just furry air cos there was so little heaviness to him and he didn't bite me this time only his claws dug a bit into my skin and I held him up to my eyes so I could look into his face and I could see that the gluey stuff had begun to go away from his eyes and little sideways slices of his eyes could be seen now and they were green, as green as the sky was blue that morning. I spoke to the kitten then in my head and said to him that he was welcome in the world and him coming into it happy'd me very much and made me better in some ways and stronger even and his eyes slowly closed the tiny bit that they were open and his claws stopped digging so hard into my skin and I put him back into the straw hole with his brothers and his sisters and he lay with them sleeping with his little sides going in-and-out cos he was alive and his tiny pointy tail flicking about a little bit. Charlesworth got down into the hole with her children and curled herself up around them and I watched them for a bit and spoke to them for a bit in my head then I heard Arrn bark and saw him below me run over all in an excitement to the gate to the yard and I looked and saw over that gate and still some way away but coming up the mountain towards Drunkle's farm a truck.

An orange truck. Like the one that Arthur would drive when he wasn't in his black one. Coming up the mountain pointed at the yard with only me and Arrn in it no flippin Drunkle what would we do what would me and Arrn do.

I shouted Arrn's name not just in my head this time but with my throat too but he didn't hear me cos of the noise of the truck so I sat down behind a bale of straw and looked. Arrn had stopped his noises and now his tail was going wag a bit which put a puzzlement on me cos he wouldn't go wag for Arthur and my heart was going bang and the truck stopped at the gate and the door opened and Rhiannon got out of the truck and my heart then went bang some more, oh yes. She put her hand over the gate and patted Arrn on the head and he wagged even more and faster then she drove the truck through the gate and parked it at the bottom of Straw Hill and she got out again and then went over to close the gate and Arrn followed her wagging and by the time she'd closed the gate and turned round I had climbed down off the straw and was standing in the yard on one of the only clean bits among all the mucksome stuff. Bang went my chest.

And hot so hot I went when she smiled at me. Smiled like the sun smiled on me all warm and Good on my face.

—Bumped into your uncle in town, she said. —Said you were up here on your own so I've come to make you some dinner. Told you I would, didn't I?

One of Them Questions. I just nodded and she sent her smile with her eyes up and down me from my boots to my head still wet from the shower and my eyes were pinned to her face like when you pin some string between the posts at the bottom of a door and hope that your NotDad will trip over it and smash his stupid head in but he sees it and kicks it away and then smacks you round the head, my eyes were pinned to her face like that string was pinned across that door. The shape she made in the bluesky air and the smell she made in my nose and Arrn was looking up at me not her and I looked down at him and he went wag but he looked a little bit worried too and the heat in me had settled in me like hot food does of a cold night-time-ness and Rhiannon fetched a bag from the truck and we walked across the mucksome yard towards the house and she was saying words to me but they just sounded like noises not Proper Words like the sound of water over stones or wind in the treeleaves lovely sounds but not Proper Words. And all I could feel was the hotness inside me and all I could smell was the skin that held Rhiannon in and all I could hear was the No Words Songs coming out of her mouth.

We went into the kitchen which still smelled of my breakfast toastness and I sat in the big old sink-inny chair by the fire which wasn't lit cos of the blueness outside and Arrn sat by me and we both watched Rhiannon as she stood and took things out of her bag. There was boots on her and jeans like mine the colour of the sky and there was a shirt on her yellow-coloured like the sun or the yolk of a fried egg and of a thinness and the light coming in through the window behind her made it go kind of invisibley in parts which sent me hotter like the fire when it was lit which it wasn't then but it didn't need to be for me to go glow. Her hair was all around her face and down her back too and dark but with shining bits in it like the bits that go gleam on top of the mountain when the sun sits on it some days. She took her rings and bangley things off her wrists and fingers and went into her bag and took out a dead rabbit not long dead cos he was still all flopsome in her hands and I saw the wires and strings moving under the skin of her hands and arms and I thought of the blood in there and my heart went bang.

—Rabbit stew. Like rabbit stew?

I nodded my head cos I did.

—Caught him this morning with the dog.

I nodded again but didn't know why I just felt my head going into a nodment. I liked to see the rabbits running up and down and across the hills and fields but I didn't mind one dying and being chopped up and eaten this way cos it wasn't like the chickens kept in wire shoeboxes in the big buildings at the end of the valley by Mr Powell, no. The rabbit had been rabbity and not in a cage and Rhiannon's dog had hunted and killed him cos That's What Dogs Do, like Arrn with the rats except we don't eat *them* yick no but if the rabbit didn't get eaten then he'd Die For No Reason and that is a terrible bad thing for a rabbit or in fact anything on the planet to do, oh yes.

Rhiannon took a big knife and a small knife too from one of the drawers. She laid Mr Rabbit flat on his back with his legs out and then she sawed off his tail and it lay there like a tiny little animal itself just a little furry ball all white. Scut, that's what rabbits' tails are called, Drunkle told me once.

—Cos you're going to need building up if you're going to take on Arthur, aren't you?

She gave a Looking and a Smiling at me and I gave a smiling back to her. She sawed through the rabbit's fur under his front legs then sawed in a circle around his neck but not so deep that his head fell off. Not much blood came out cos he'd probably already been cut in the neck to let the blood out cos that's what you have to do when you're going to eat a thing you've just killed. But there was *some* blood of course and it kind of jumped out and went across the backs of Rhiannon's hands in red lines and one bit jumped up on to her arm and I looked at it all so red against her skin which wasn't red but not really white either kind of the colour of the pollen that the bees carry in little bags on their legs on days like that day all in a bluesome brightness all over the place.

—Talk of the pub last night, you were. Everyone was going on and on about how brave you were, standing up to Arthur like that. Course, *he* went on and on about teaching you a lesson but we all just ignored him. He knocked you out, didn't he? Grown man doing that to a kid, Christ. Coward. No one listened to a single word he said and he just went off in a strop round about midnight. Haven't seen him since.

She gave me another Smiling and I saw the long-ness of her fingers and the shiny nails all the same sharpness and I watched them dig into the rabbit's fur and dig in further into his neck. One hand grabbed his head to hold it still cos it was moving around even tho it wasn't alive any more and the other hand that was in the neck grabbed tight hold of his fur and started to pull it down and off and it made a quiet kind of rippy noise all wet and sticky and as the fur came off I saw the stuff beneath all kind of shiny and purple and bulgesome. Rhiannon ripped the fur down more to Mr Rabbit's back legs then she took up the small knife and made some cuts at them legs then pulled the fur down even more and then quickly it came off like a jumper, like jumpers I take off when days get bright and bluesome only not so bloody as Mr Rabbit's clothes. It looked like Rhiannon was then wearing red gloves up to her elbows but not just of One Redness they were all kinds of a redness almost black even in parts and they went even more colours when she cut open Mr Rabbit's belly and wiggled some of her fingers inside in their longness and she pulled out all tubes and bags and sacks all slimesome and smellbad and going all of a slobber as if they were alive too like worms or slugs or things you sometimes find at the edge of the sea, when you lift rocks and look under.

—Daft bastard's convinced himself that your dog's been killing his sheep. Won't listen to reason that man. He gets an idea in his head and there's nothing anyone can do to get it out of there.

She put the skin and tail into a Safeway bag and then tied that bag and put it in the bin and then she took the board with all the guts and stuff on it in a dripment and slobberment to the back door and tipped it all out into the yard and Arrn watched her then legged it out there to be with the guts. I looked at the rabbit all without his skin now and not like a rabbit any more really except for his head but Rhiannon then chopped that off too and put it in the bin as well and I thought of what Rhiannon might look like under her skin and if she had the shining purpleness and all them bags and tubes inside of her too and if I did as well but of course we did cos we were alive on the mountain as well as the rabbits and without them sliming things we wouldn't be but then I thought that bees don't have those things and they're alive as much as I am so it's not just them wet things that make people alive it's something else that no one can see that fills our heads and our bodies with a lifeness. It comes out of the sky and the streams and it lets us be alive on the mountain and everywhere else too.

I could hardly see any of the skin on Rhiannon's arms, so red they had become. I was still hot inside but the banging had gone but it came back a bit when I looked at Rhiannon's arms and thought of her like a buzzard or a fox or a stoat cos they eat and chop up rabbits too only not with knives.

—It turned sour very quick with Arthur, Rhiannon said and it was as if she was talking not to me but to the dead and chopped-up rabbit. The big knife went up and then down and the dead rabbit started to go into chunks. Arrn came back into the kitchen with a redness all around his mouth and on his nose and he lay down by the fire there and he licked his paws which were a bit red too but not as much as his face. —He's a bad man. A bad human being. He's not right. I realised that soon after I married him but by then it was too late. Angharad was inside me.

She looked at me with her eyes all big as if I'd said something that put a surprise in her but no words had come out of my mouth.

—I've sent Angharad away, she said. —Packed her off to my sister's in Swansea. She'll be safe there. Arthur thinks she's gone to stay with some friends over in England, not that he could give much of a shit anyway.

She turned to the sink and made some water fall and put her hands and arms into it and rubbed them together til the redness went and the proper colour of her skin came back. The water came off the mountain and through pipes and out of the taps and Rhiannon let it take the rabbitred off her hands and arms and when her hands and arms were skin-coloured again she took down a big pot from a hook on the beam above the fireplace and the pawlicky Arrn and she tipped all the rabbit bits off the board and into that pot and then she put some water into it and put it on the cooker and she made a small blue fire happen underneath it then she washed the rabbitred off the kitchen parts too and out of her bag she took some carrots and potatoes and leeks and onions and a swede like a rock and some of that stringy green plant that comes in bunches and looks like the ribs of foxes in the snow-times only green. She did things to the plants with the small knife then chopped them too and put them in the pot with the already-chopped rabbit parts then she took some bunches of leaves from the bag all of a deep green-ness like good, good grass and she chopped them too and potted them as well and then she opened some wine the colour that her arms had gone before when she took Mr Rabbit's skin off and she poured some of that into the pot and then she put salt and pepper in and a lid on. Then she just stood for a bit and put a Looking on me then she picked up a wooden spoon and took the lid off the pot and stirred the stuff in it with that spoon.

—Christ, we make some mistakes. Bad, bad mistakes. But how can we do anything else? We only get one chance at this. Fuck up once and you fuck up for ever.

And it was like she said them words to the rabbit bits and the plant bits cos she was looking down into the pot at them as she spoke and then she put the lid back on the pot with a clang and she turned and put another Smiling on me and held her hands together at her tummy and I liked very much her Smiling and I liked very much her hands held together at her tummy like that and I liked very much her hair and her skin now not red and the drawy-inny way her eyes went then.

—Couple of hours and that'll be ready, she said. — What shall we do til then?

I had a Big Thinking in my head of what we could do just me and Rhiannon til the stew was ready to eat and it was something that I hadn't done before not in Real Life anyway only in my head altho that is part of Real Life too of course and it had to do with my hands going on parts of Rhiannon's body and her hands going on parts of mine and bits of me going hot and hard and at that Big Thinking some bits of me *did* go hard and hot and I felt my face go red like Rhiannon's hands and arms did with the blood before. Again she put a big Smiling on me and I went redder and hotter and harder and to make the pictures in my head go away I thought of the little bitey black-and-white kitten but it was not like I *meant* to think about him he just came into my head. So I told Rhiannon about him and she said why don't you show him to me so I said yes and stood and Arrn looked at me just once then fell back into sleep again by the fire that wasn't lit but maybe it was in his head and that was Good Enough for him.

Rhiannon took the bottle of wine with her and we went out into the muckiness of the yard and the bright blue aboveness and across the dirtsome yard and into the barn and up the strawbale hill and we sat down and looked into the hole and saw Charlesworth on her side with her babies sucking at her and she was going prrr, prrr and she looked at us with one green eye and made a kind of smiley face the way that cats do sometimes a bit like people even. My little black-and-white feller was in there sucking away and Rhiannon made nice noises at Charlesworth and her children and told her what a clever cat she was and how beautiful her babies were and we sat like that for a bit looking at Charlesworth and her babies and the Good Smell came off Rhiannon and into my nose and I liked it and my head had stopped its banging and my face had stopped its hotting and the hardness in my middle body had gone too and I was gladded by that cos I knew what that hardness would make happen after a while, how shakey my legs would go and the world would become nothing but the niceness in me when stuff would come out and that would be the Best Feeling Ever even better than just before My Times are about to happen. I still felt a bit firesome Down There cos of Rhiannon's nearness but the hardness had gone away and yes I was gladded by that in a way but had a bit of a sadness on me too cos it would've been nice if Rhiannon herself had made that hardness go and the Best Feeling Ever come.

We watched Charlesworth and her children for a bit then we moved away a bit from her into a space where some bales had been taken away and had made a kind of flat bit like a bed. We sat on that flat bit with our backs up against a kind of bale-shelf so we could see over the edge and into the yard below and further over that the road coming up the mountain and the mountain top too of course with the sun going down slowly to sit and shine on it. Rhiannon drank some of the wine then she passed the bottle to me and even tho I'd never drunk wine before I took the bottle and drank some down and it was like the taste of it had always been in me since before I was born when I was waiting up there in the starness for my birthing and my beingness and my aliveness up here in the High Parts. It was like the wine was a part of me that had been missing and like the glass of the bottle touching my lips and the softness of the wine inside my head and body was Always Meant To Be.

—Go easy. You don't want to end up like your uncle.

No I thought I do not want my sheep shot or my wife to become a branch but I didn't have a wife or sheep so I wondered what she meant. I wanted to ask her what she meant but then she took the bottle back from me and put it to her lips and I watched her lips the colour of plums bulge out around the glass O end of the bottle and I felt the hardness coming back into the middle bits of me again and I didn't know why only that I liked the way her lips went around the end of that bottle. We sat like that with the bottle going between us and Rhiannon's lips going all bulgey until all the wine had gone inside us making us tell each other stories and I told Rhiannon of My Times and of what I see in them and I told her of the Everything-thing and the Lordy fellers and of Auntie Fay still somehow being alive somewhere and become something else and Rhiannon told me of her fears for Angharad and I told her of the waiting sadness of the world and she told me of how Arthur's sperm in her is like the poison of an adder and that put a shock-ness and a sickness into me and then she started to talk about there being a purity in me and I thought of that in there all going glow like the wine altho I didn't really know what she meant and I asked her and she said that it was Good and Solid and alive in me like it was in No Other and I didn't know what she meant still but then I kind of did because all in a sudden I felt a Goodness and an Aliveness in me cos Rhiannon's hand was on me, grabbing the hardness in my middle and I felt my body go open like a flower or a weed on a pond and then I felt nothing at all or no that's not right then I *thought* of nothing at all cos

I was just doing things that felt Good and Right and Proper like the taste and the feeling of the wine or like when I watch the morning-times come across the mountain or like in My Times when I don't have a Thinking in my head just a Doing in my bodyness and It is alive in me and me on the mountain and the mountain on the planet and the planet a blue-green pea in space and it was something I'd never done before but it was like I'd never stopped doing it so easy was it all.

Hands on heads and faces. Mouths going together all soft and mashy together and tongues around each other like eels in the lake when they make other eels. Hands on clothes all yanky and draggy and then clean blue air on skin like water without a wetness and mouths on bits of that skin making those bits go gluey and warm and tingly like fingers and toes put in front of a fire after being put in snow. Salty tastes and sweetness tastes and tastes like nothing ever else. Fingers going gentle into little sticky caves and moving around gentle in those caves and when I put my mouth over Rhiannon's caves and my tongue in them to taste them she shouted no words just made shouts that went out over the mountain and the tastes in my mouth were of meat and salt and sugar and fish and jam and bread and herbs and corn and milk. I went on her like the kittens were going on Charlesworth and Rhiannon went on me like that too only on a different bodybit and I lay back in a flatness with my arms going out and I felt the mountain move beneath me and it was like My Tmes a bit cos it was all changing me and making me different and I was growing in it and as happy'd as I could ever be. Rhiannon's legs went each side of me and she moved up my body and I could see her face just above mine but so near with her hair hanging down in a curtain-ness and her eyes closed and her mouth open a little bit to show toothybits and she leaned back and reached under and made us slot together like a gate into a latch and in that coming togetherment everything else came together, it did, Everything In The World, all its badness and goodness and sadness and happiness all went together and made One Thing not Good and not Bad either just One Whole Thing that was Just There and it was like I was flying above it all to see it in its One-ness me and Rhiannon going so high to see it all and it being just there beneath us locked together as we were like that and Rhiannon squeezing me tight to her and me squeezing her tight to me and nothing bad could break us apart so very very tight was our squeezing and then in that Best Feeling Ever both of us turning into an Everything-ness cos it was like bursting open like a cloud too full of rain and the happiness on me was bigger than the mountain and Rhiannon rolled off me and lay at my side and our breathings went like an engine and I wanted Nothing More. Felt I could fly with her off me but that might've been because of Something Else not just the new not-heaviness I didn't know.

The roaring beast on the mountain top and the sheep He takes up trees. Like that snake that swallowed the frog and the frog's feet going all flappy. Like Arrn and the rats and the buzzards and the rabbits and the fox and the moorhens and like everything

everything from the mountain in its bigness to the tiny bits of lifeness on every leaf that your eye can Only Just See and even those things that you can't see cos they're much too small or are invisible like the wind but you still know they're there around you cos you can feel them on your face or you can hear them Call Your Name. Like the owls in the trees in the night-time-ness or them jellyish things at the bottoms of ponds and all the things that Call Your Name, oh yes.

Rhiannon's hand went flat and soft on my belly and I jumped a little bit cos it was a bit of a shock and I thought she might be wanting to Go Together with me again and I would've done It too but she just let out a little bit of a laughing and then she gave me some words:

—That was your first time, wasn't it?

Nod nod yes.

—So now you'll never forget me. You never forget your first one. I'll always be in you now, in here.

She put a patting on the bit of my body where my heart was going beat and she patted it twice like I do on Arrn's head and I heard it go boom boom inside of me. My head went flopsome to the side to look at her but she wasn't looking at me she was giving a Smiling to the roof of the barn and I saw her give a nod in answer to no question unless it was one that she asked herself. Then she said that we'd better get dressed and Go Inside and so we did that and I felt a bit sadded when our clothes had gone back on and I couldn't see Rhiannon's skin anymore or her bulge-some bits or fursome bits and nor could she see mine,

Hidden we were again from each other and I felt a sad feeling that a Good Time had gone and I would never have it again. Then we said tara to Charlesworth and her children who were all in a sleeping with their sides going in and out cos they were alive and then we climbed down off the straw hill and went across the mucksome yard back towards the house and Just In Time too cos I heard the truck of Drunkle coming up the mountain but we were inside before he could see us together in the kitchen that smelled then of Good Things which put a thunderment in my belly and made spit go into my mouth and Arrn was sitting up and looking at us and going wag and we heard the truck turn off outside and a door close and Rhiannon put her lips on mine just once and then put a Looking on me and I could not stop myself from hotting and harding when I saw my face tiny in her eyes. She put her finger to them lips and made a shushy sound and nodded a question at me and I nodded answerly back at her cos I Understood. Not to tell Drunkle, that was in her shushing and questiony nodment, not to tell my Drunkle about our Going Together and I Understood that and so went nod nod and gave her a smiling then the kitchen door opened and my Drunkle came in.

—Rhiannon. What're you doing here?

—Making some stew for you and the boy. Hungry?

He stood in the doorway and sent a sniffing around the room then he smiled at everything in that room and I was gladded to see him smile cos he's my Drunkle.

—Starving, aye. And that smells just the job.

He turned that smiling on me then put a ruffle-
ment in my hair with his hand and I gave a smiling
back to him and he sat in the old sink-inny armchair
by the fire which wasn't lit and Arrn's head went up
a bit and his tail went wag and Drunkle put a ruffle-
ment on his head too then Arrn fell back into his
sleeping and looked dead happy cos everything was
Right and Proper for him he was in the middle of
people he liked and made him go wag. Drunkle took
his boots off and waggled his toes in his socks and
said that he'd Bought Some Things To Clean Up The
Yard With, bags and spades and brushes and things,
and that he was going to use them after he'd eaten
something cos he was starving and that wasn't like
him cos he's my Drunkle. Rhiannon was taking things
over to the table, bread and bowls and things, and I
was watching her move and the swayment in her legs
and hips and the way her bum bulged twicely under
her jeans and the other bulges on her body and her
hair and the jangley bangley things around her wrists
but she didn't look at me back but I could tell that
she knew I was looking cos I saw her small smilings
and saw her eyes flick once at me fast like the swal-
lows and swifts that were swooshing and flicking around
the yard and house and mountain then cos that's what
they do, them birds, in the summernesses. Rhiannon
said for us to sit at the table and we did and Arrn
carried on sleeping cos he'd already eaten, them rabbit
guts were in his guts and that put a puzzling on me
to have some guts inside other guts like when motor-
bikes get put on the backs of trucks it makes me laugh
a little bit. Arrn slept upside down on his back with

his legs in a dangling all four and his lips hanging down nearly to his eyes which fell open a little bit upside down to watch Rhiannon bring bowls of stew over to us and a good smellsome steam came up off and out of them and Drunkle put his face into that steam and sniffed and went 'aaahhh' and then Rhiannon sat with us too with her own steamsome bowl and we put our spoons into the stew and raised them and put the lovely lovely stew inside our bodies.

That lovely lovely stew. Thank you Mr Rabbit for the lovely lovely stew and thank you Rhiannon too not just for that stew but for making in me the Best Time Ever I will never ever forget it, no. I ate the rabbit and the vegetables and the stewjuice and looked over at Rhiannon blowing on the tiny pond of stew in her spoon her plum lips going out like they did at the wine bottle and I wanted again to mash my lips on hers and feel her lips again on my bodyparts and wondered if again I ever would. She spoke to Drunkle about Arthur and other things to do with 'business' and 'money' which made me feel all of a flatness inside so I let myself think about what I'd just done with Rhiannon in the straw and of course that made me Hot and Hard again so when I'd eaten my stew and some bread I went up the stairs and lay on my bed and put my hand on Myself and made another Good Time happen but it wasn't as good as it had been with Rhiannon but it made the Hotness and Hardness go away which I was happy'd by cos then I could think of other things again. Then I looked at Bala Lake for a bit but saw no monster only some people sitting outside a caravan and eating chips out of the paper and some time later I heard a truck start up and I looked out of the window and saw Rhiannon in the orange truck go driving away from the house and off the mountain and I was sadded and inside me it felt like there was a fish biting on a hook. Drunkle shouted my name so I went down the stairs to him and he went to ask me something but before he could get the words out I asked him where Rhiannon had gone.

—Ach, she's gone home to that caveman husband of hers. He'll be coming in off the fields soon and wanting his tea and woe betide that poor woman if it isn't on the table. She took a pan of stew with her so at least she won't have to cook anything for the idle bastard.

He put a bit of a Looking on me and I put a bit of a Looking on him and there was a small Smiling on him too but only a Very Small One.

—Anyway. Fancy helping your uncle clean up his farmyard?

I nodded yes cos I *did* so we both went and put some old clothes on that we didn't mind getting dirty and we went outside into the blueness of the day and I just looked at everything around me at all the empty bags and broken machine parts and piles of poo and mucksome puddles and DuwDuw I thought, where the blinking heck should I start? So I just stood there in a stillness looking around and Drunkle went around the barn where the machines that worked were kept and I heard an engine start up and then I heard Arrn go woof inside the house as if he was answering that rumblesome engine and then Drunkle came back around the barn driving the small tractor, the brown one with no cab on it but with the bucket fixed on. We took up all the Stuff That Wasn't Muck and brushed a corner clear and put all that stuff in that corner into a big pile of bags and metal like a skeleton or a car crash or something and then we brushed and spaded all the muckstuff into piles and it stank and ran and was horrible and white worms went wriggle in it and other things with lots of legs ran and jumped away and flies went whining and it was all yicksome and all the time I was thinking about Rhiannon's skin and her bulgey bits and her little warm wet caves and how it felt when she touched me and put her mouth on me and I wanted her to Do It Again. Drunkle used the bucket on the tractor to shovel up all the piles of muckiness then he tipped it all in the midden then we loaded all the bags and broken stuff into the bucket and he took it and tipped it behind the barn and said that we'd take it to the tip tomorrow or the day after or sometime soon anyway and then we cleaned out the pigs or no *we* didn't cos I took them into another pen and scratched them with a stick which they loved and Drunkle used the small tractor to take all the poo and stuff out into the midden with all the other muck-iness and then he put clean straw into the pigpen and I opened the gate for them to get back in there and they did and went all runny and kicky as if they liked the clean-ness around them which I think they did cos pigs aren't dirty even tho loads of people say and think that they are. Then we poured Jeyes fluid and other bleachy stuff all over the yard and we brushed it and brushed it and brushed it and then squirted water all over it with a hose and by that time the blueness had gone out of the sky but the blackness wasn't in it yet and we stood in the poo-gone, clean-smellsome yard and watched the bats flapping around us so fast and I liked standing there like that, achey and all in a tiredness as night-time went into the sky and the bats danced around my head and all around me was Clean and Good. Except for me, of course, I wasn't clean cos some muck had gone on me and Drunkle too so we went back into the house and put our horrible clothes in the washing machine and then we both had showers and ate some more of Rhiannon's stew with big pieces of bread and Arrn ate some too and we watched the telly but not for very long cos we were all Dead Tired after making the yard clean and so we went to bed and I lay on the bed in the darkness with Arrn below me under the bed and I thought of Rhiannon and put a touching on Myself again and made another Good Time happen which put an even bigger tiredness on me and my eyes went all heavy and droopsome and just before I went off into a sleeping I heard an owl outside in the yard, outside in the world that I had made All Clean and that now had mine and Rhiannon's Going Together in it and all of that happy'd me and so I fell asleep happy, oh yes.

And the summer went by into the Rainy Times and the days rose into a bluesome brightness then fell again into a warm darkness, rise and fall and rise and fall that's what the days did and the summerness went into me all green and foamsome in places and in other places brown like the gravy Teifi, sometimes all bright like when the sun sits on the mountain top which it did a lot and sometimes darker like the water in the lakes or the river and I was *on* and *in* the mountain. Me and Arrn ran in a Good Madness across the High Parts and through the yard that Drunkle kept clean and I Kept An Eye Out for the ghost of the bull Snowball but didn't see it altho one time Arrn came running out of the cowshed with his eyes all big and the hairs on his back all sticky-uppy. Charlesworth's kittens grew up and got big and we had to Get Rid Of Them, so Drunkle and me made a sign with white paint on some wood that said 'KITTENS – FREE TO GOOD HOMES' and people stopped in their cars and took some kittens, all of them in fact except for the little black-and-white feller which I was gladded by cos he was the best one and Charlesworth didn't seem upset by her children going and then one day she herself had gone, she just wasn't in the straw one morning and she never came back. She went to open up a shop on the other side of the mountain or went to be with the Beast in the storm and Drunkle said to me don't be sad cos that's Just What Cats Do. There are foxes and badgers and other toothed things out there on the mountain. The black-and-white feller grew bigger but never really got very big cos that wasn't for him and he set up his own house in the straw and every day I'd go to see him and stroke him and he'd go prrrr and wouldn't bite me any more. I never had My Times again all through the summerness altho I did think I was going to two times but I didn't, not while the sun shone in a bluesome brightness anyway which it did all through that summer.

Rhiannon came to visit us a lot and I went Hot and Hard whenever she did but we never Went Together again even tho I wanted to all the time and hoped we would again and she gave me Smilings a lot which was her way of telling me that she remembered what we did in the straw and that she liked to remember it but that we wouldn't do it again, all of that was in her Smilings. I puzzled about it a lot and thought about it a lot and spoke to Arrn about it but never Drunkle and at times I wanted a Time so I could ask Auntie Scantie Fay about it but My Times never came that summer in the bluesome brightness, no. But I would watch Rhiannon and wish for her Smilings and feel good whenever she gave them to me and I wondered why we never Went Together again if she didn't want to Go Together with me then why did she do it that one time or maybe she didn't like doing it with me but I knew that she did cos I remembered the way her face went and the noises she made oh! oh! like that. And then one night-time, just me and Arrn on the hill with all the stars about us and above us *on* the mountain and the mountain *in* us and I had a quick knowing all of a sudden of how sometimes people Need To Do Things cos they think about them things a lot and parts of their insideness go wriggle like eels until they do those things and it might only need to happen once to stop them eels wriggling and after that Once there is no need to do that thing again and maybe that's what happened with Rhiannon and me. And I was okay with that thinking I wasn't sadded by it no it was okay. But I did look at Rhiannon every time she came up to the farm and I liked looking at her but I started to worry about Arthur and what would be Going Through His Head cos she was up at the farm a lot and four times I thought I saw Arthur's black truck parked far away on the Other Peak and other times I thought a saw a Bright Flash like when the sun puts a shining down to bounce off glass on that Other Peak but I thought that it might've been some kind of glassy rock up there and not binoculars cos there are such rocks like glass up there so I didn't worry about it and in the meanwhile Rhiannon moved about the yard and through the house and I couldn't stop myself putting a Looking on her. A Looking and a Smiling and oh yes a Wanting.

No more sheep got killed by the Beast if that is really what was happening to them. The Beast died or went away or started killing other things cos no more sheep got found up trees or anywhere else made dead by rips or teeth or whatever it had been. NotDad never went away but Duw I wanted him to, wanted the Beast to rip his stupid bastard head off but that never happened but My Mam Bethan *did* come up to the farm to see me and one time she brought me My Pills which I never needed or took cos My Times weren't on me then and she also brought me up some biscuits which I did need cos they were my Very Favourite Types. We sat at the table outside by the house and she drank tea and smoked and I ate the good, good biscuits and I can't remember what we spoke about only that she told me I was happy where I was and to stay there and I understood what she meant and didn't want to go back Down There anyway with her and bastard NotDad cos I was better Up

There in the High Parts with Drunkle and Arrn and the black-and-white cat and Rhiannon when she was around which wasn't Always but was A Lot and Drunkle asked My Mam Bethan if she wanted to stay over for tea or go for a drink in the Mountain Tavern but she said no, she Had To Get Back and I watched her go fast off the mountain back to bastard NotDad and she moved fast in a panic-ment like a woodlouse when you lift a rock and they go mad trying to find the darkness again and run at another rock, that's how My Mam Bethan went off the mountain and I didn't like to see her moving like a woodlouse so I turned away and whistled for Arrn and he came and we both then went running off to climb Straw Hill but not like woodlouses oh no. Bag of flour please Charlesworth oh no you're not there. Any more.

Drunkle was my Drunkle sometimes but mostly he was just my Uncle which I was happy'd by cos he's my Drunkle but he wasn't then, most of the time. Drunkle or Uncle I loved him both. He didn't talk about Auntie Fay a lot but I knew he could remember her and feel her and smell her cos I could too and sometimes his eyes would go close but not in a sleep-ment and I knew that he was back with Auntie Fay when he went like that. Sometimes Rhiannon and him would Go Off Together and I wondered if they were properly Going Together but they weren't I don't think because there wasn't that nice cloud around them or those Smilings between them which come off people who Go Together In That Way except My Mam Bethan and NotDad cos NotDad's a bastard man and the cloud around them two is black and it stinks like the mud

me and Drunkle spaded out of the yard and like that
cloud around face-scrapey Arthur and Rhiannon at
the beginning of the summer when the Beast was on
the mountain cos the nice cloud was around me and
Rhiannon for a bit but the summer burned it away
like it burns the mist off the mountain in the morning-
times and that sadded me for a bit but I didn't really
mind cos there would always for ever be a little bit
of that Good Cloud around me and Rhiannon and I
was mostly happy'd by that. And in fact most of the
days of that summer happy'd me I had No School and
no My Times I was *on* the mountain and I swam with
Arrn in the lakes and streams in the High Parts and
sometimes with Drunkle and Rhiannon too and our
skin went like a chicken's with its feathers taken out
and we found a fish in a suit of armour like a Knight
Of Old which Rhiannon told me was a Crayfish and
I picked him up to have a close look at him and I
liked him very much and saw his eyes and claws and
kicking feet he was like some kind of insectfish but
big. I watched the kites fly like Jesus's cross in the
bluesome brightsome sky and the buzzards too and I
spent ages watching a harrier hover and I found that
same bird's nest when I was walking just a patch of
mud in the bogness which smelled very bad and had
all bones in it and I could see a chick in the ryegrass
all in a huddlement so I went away quick from it cos
I didn't want to make it scared and didn't want to be
divebombed by its mum and dad with their speedy
claws and beaks, oh no. I saw an adder on a stone and
woke him up but didn't mean to and his tongue came
out all flicky-flicky and he made a noise like when

Drunkle has to let air out of a tyre and he jumped at us so fast with his mouth open and his fangs so sudden sharp and me and Arrn ran away. I sat on a hill on my own with no Arrn, he was left woofing back in the house cos he would've scared the badgers that I was spying on and the sun went down all red and orange behind the mountain and I saw one badger come out of the trees then another one then three smaller ones too and I watched them for ages all five as they played and went into tumblements down the hill my family of little black-and-white bears. I watched the black-and-white cat hunt for rats in the farmyard and didn't mind cos That's What Cats Do and I stood still in the yard as the night-time-ness came into the sky and fell down around me and the bats went flit and flick around my head and so close to me. All of the world was *on* me and *in* me and I was happy happy happy like that tiny bit of time I have before I have a My Time, it was like I was nothing but everything just part of the snakey birdy batty world around me and my blood went in me like a river and my brain in my head was like a cloud with the sun bright in it and the days all blue and green and foamsome like a stream going around rocks and I thought of people like me who Had My Blood so many many years ago living on the mountain and turning rocks into tools like Drunkle showed me that time and sometimes it felt like I would burst with the Thinking of that and the Knowing of it and the light that came out of everything and went *in* me I sometimes felt like I was in a Heaven that summer cos so very many things happened and I was happy-happy-*happy'd* by them all but then the world moved around in space the bluegreen pea planet spun in the blackness and the brightness went and the blueness went and a bit of the warmness stayed in the air but the sky went dark and the clouds came all of a greyness and of a rain-some weight and the thin rain came down to the world all around me and that was then the Bad Thing happened, oh yes.

There was a storm on the mountain and we went out to look at it, me and Drunkle and Rhiannon and Arrn. We had slippy coats on which would Keep The Rain Off, well Arrn didn't he just had his fur, and the storm was all purple-flashy above and behind the mountain and rumbling and lightning like the hands of giant white skeletons kept coming down to make a grab at the top of the mountain and then go away again so very very quick. We stood in the yard still clean and watched it and when it moved away from that mountain top we got into Drunkle's truck all four of us and drove after it fast cos such an amazement it put in us and we wanted to see it more and be in it too and when I looked at it all in its madness close to me on the mountain top I felt like I'd gone to the place where Auntie Fay had gone and that I'd turned like her too into something new and strong that Knew Everything. So we drove up into the Even Higher Parts then past the Tavern and down a bit into lower parts and we were all happy and laughing cos we were Chasing The Storm and Arrn was going woof in a good way and the sky was going dark as the night-ness began to eat it which made the storm look Even

Better and my heart and head were Going Like Mad
and I think Drunkle's were too and Rhiannon's as
well and Arrn's also cos of all the Happy Noises all of
us were making. We drove in to the bottom of the
valley and got out of the car and put our wellies on
except Arrn of course and walked out on to the squishsome bit all of us looking up at the sky going FLASH
and BOOM and how great that was and I knew where
we were on that squishsome ground we were going
towards the Hole and the Fountain and the Standing
Stones and Arrn was jumping around and going
wagwagwag and Drunkle kept pointing up at the sky
and them giant white skeleton's hands kept pointing
down at us with fingers all thin and big and bone-
some and I had a hood up over my head and the rain
on it was going:
drumdrumdrumdrumdrum.
drumdrumdrumdrumdrum.
And I felt my eyes go rolling and I could nearly see
my brain with them backwards-going-eyes. I tried not
to listen to the drumdrum noise of the rain but it was
filling my head around my ears cos of the hood so I
took the hood off but that was no good in fact it was
worse cos then the rain went drumdrumdrumdrumdrum on my skull and made it go wet as well. My
eyes were going back. My eyes kept going back. Arrn
was looking at me in a worryness but Drunkle and
Rhiannon were ahead of me closer to the storm and
all in an excitement because of that storm and they
were drinking from a bottle of wine which they'd
started to do back at the house like me and Rhiannon
did The Time We Went Together and which Drunkle

always used to do but which he hadn't done for ages and I shouted out both their names but the storm wouldn't let them hear me and my eyes kept going back.

Drunkle and Rhiannon went off and around the squishsome bit and I followed them with Arrn. The Hole was close by me but I didn't quite know where cos of the darkly creeping and the Fountain and the Stones were close by too but I couldn't see them either I just knew they were there. I shouted The Names again but my voice was smaller than a fly's voice in that boomboom thunder and drumdrum rain. My eyes were going back.

I looked down at the ground for feathers or bones or anything like that but could see none so I pulled some moss up instead off a rock and tucked it behind my ear and wetness from it went in a tricklement into my ear which was already wet anyway but it was different in its wetness cos it made my head go funny all kind of wobbly and flopsome like mud and the mountain around me that I was *on* and *in* went flop from side to side. Bad taste sicky feeling in my mouth It was going to happen They were coming oh God.

—Drunkle . . . Rhiannon . . .

FLASH and I saw them in that FLASH standing by the Stones as if for a shelterment that wasn't there and the four of them like that looked like four stones all standing together even tho only two of them were stones and they looked like some writing or sign from the sky that drumdrum. Everything Going Together.

Yes

Everything going into

Owl: white ghost barn owl skimming through the rain and I watched him and he flew past close and watched me and I couldn't see his eyes cos of the rain and the coming darkness but still I felt myself going into those eyes and then the body of that bird and then I was looking out through Owl's eyes high above it all could feel the rain making my wings go heavy and I looked down and I saw

Me and Arrn standing by the Hole like a big black O next to us and the stream going into the fountain fuller and faster cos of the rain and the Stones below me, all of it below me cos I was in Owl and I was flying, yes I was flying again, them two Stones small down there and Rhiannon and Drunkle standing by them gone small too and behind their backs in a red coat Arthur hunched over creeping towards them and in his hand an axe.

—UNCLE! RHIANNON!

I shouted in Owl's voice which they didn't know so they didn't do anything but stand there in the storm so Owl sent me out from him and back into me and Arrn was woofing and all was dark again I could see Nothing just the rain in silver lines. I tried to run but everything was wobblesome and I fell on my arse with a splash in the squishy stuff which was bad and my legs wouldn't work I couldn't stand all I could do was sit there wet and shout.

—UNNNNCLE! UNNNNCLE!

Voice gone gulped by the voices from the sky so loud with the booming breaking my head and FLASH and I saw:

Creeping Arthur

RhiannonandDrunkle

Them looking up at the rage in the sky and putting a Smiling at that angerment but I couldn't see their faces just their backs and another FLASH and:

Creeping Arthur

RhiannonandDrunkle

And I screamed their names as loud as I could so loud it hurt my throat or no it wasn't their Proper Names just a very loud noise I made but that is the name of everybody really it's not what people call you or what you write on papers and forms or anything like that it's just a Noise that is Your Name it is the Name Of The World just that No-Word Noise in the watersome darkness and FLASH again and I saw Rhiannon was in the mud on the floor and Arthur was going chop chop with the axe like a butcher does and Drunkle was on Arthur's back and then it was dark again but shadows now just dark shapes I could see and one arm in red with an axe in it going up and down and terrible screams I could hear through the drumdrum rain.

Some sick came out of me then and made more squishsome the stuff I was sitting in. Wobblement wobblement everywhere and the mountain gone soft and me not standing and Drunkle and Rhiannon getting chopped by Arthur over there by the Stones and I felt then a rough warmness on my face and my eyes came back and I looked and saw Arrn's nose so close cos he was licking my face and I saw his eyes like pools and I saw Auntie Fay somewhere in them so I went into them like I'd gone into Owl's and then I was Arrn my good dog Arrn and I ran in leapings over the wet world and I jumped and I felt such a powerness in my legs and neck and a hardness in my teeth and I could see through the silver rain and the falling nightness and I saw Drunkle all crumpled at the bottom of one of the Stones where it rose up out of the ground and his eyes were closed and there was blood on his face from a slit in his head and I saw the axe go up and I saw one of Rhiannon's hands go in front of her face but it didn't really look like a hand any more cos of the finger-gone-ness of it and I heard Arthur roar out of his red beard that fell down in rainy ropes on to the front of his red jacket:

—FUCKING WHORE! THINK I'M FUCKING STUPID, WOMAN? ALL FUCKING SUMMER? THINK I DIDN'T KNOW? SHOULD'VE DONE THIS YEARS AGO, YOU TWISTED SICK –

The hand up there holding the axe and bloodstripes on that hand and that axe and about to bring the axe down again and I felt myself leave the earth and then felt that hand between my teeth and then felt a crunching boneness in my teeth and I heard a scream and nothing could make me stop biting that hand, yank YANK went the hand to get away but I bit down even harder and then a bloodtaste happened and I felt a hardness in my teeth so I bit down even harder but then I felt whackings on my side and head and felt and heard some crunchings happening there too so I moved away from them whackings and the hand went out of my mouth. I looked up and saw Arthur holding his wrist with his other hand in the silver lines of rain and he had no axe then and blacker wetness was coming out of his hand and I jumped at him again but not like with my legs it was as if the mountain threw me off it at Arthur and I saw his neck coming fast and I snapped with my jaws but missed that neck and when I landed he landed on me with his knee pressed into my neck and my face in the squishsome mud and sinking into the mudness and all that mudness in my eyes and nose and ears my face being forced deeper. Deeper. Deeper into the earth and everything in that mudness then went into me too all the bones of My People Gone and the stones they used and their houses now long gone into the soil all the many hundred years of it, all that life on the mountain leading towards one thing which was the birthing of me and the more of that mud that went into me the stronger I got and I could feel myself my dog-body going bigger and stronger almost bursting with the strongness and I pushed myself down even deeper into the mud where Arthur's knee could not follow and so I could eel-move out from under him and stand and then I could see him and he was putting a Looking on me and the mountain gave a shrug and threw me at his face again and I heard myself roar like the Beast like the Storm and he roared too but not as loud and my teeth went together SNAP and Arthur was up and running and I chased him with my own roaring so loud in my ears even louder than the storm I was and I felt the mountain kind of bunch itself up under my paws ready to throw me yet again and I just let it do that and then I was in the air and I landed on Arthur's red running back that axey nasty face-scrapey bastard and he fell forwards with me riding on his back and biting his head and down we both fell but not *on* the ground

no we went *in* the ground, *in* the hole like a big black
O and as I went down into that O I saw just for a
moment in one quick FLASH my Other Body sitting
in the sinksome mud with eyes open like the windows
of a house with no one at home and then there was
nothing but darkness whooshing past my red red ears
which had happened before but that time I was going
up and now I was going

   down

   down

   down

into the earth and everything was quiet just that soft
whooshing. Still holding on to Arthur with my paws
and teeth I could feel his Terror like heat and smell
it too like a septic tank. We both fell joined together
into the mountain and it was like I was going home
so happy did I feel and calm was I as if the mountain
wrapped its arms around me and the blackness in that
hole wasn't a Bad Blackness cos I could see through
it even, could see the circle of mucksome water with
the moon in it far below but getting quickly bigger
as we fell fast towards it and I knew that when I landed
it would be Warm and Good and everything would
be happy and fine when I was in it but just when I
was nearly in it and so close I could even smell its
niceness I went

   out

and started to go back up again and I saw Arthur
and Arrn below me go into that water and I saw the
splash and that O of water got smaller cos I was quickly
going Up and I saw Arthur come up out of that water
with his hands dragging at the slimesome stone sides

of the hole and then I saw Arrn come up out of the water too and bite Arthur's hand that he'd already bitten and he dragged him back down under the water and then I was back up into the black part of the hole and I couldn't see and noises started coming in again, screamings from Rhiannon and boomings from the sky and the drumdrumdrumdrum of the rain and then I was back *out* of the mountain and *on* it again not *in* it and everything was so loud and wet all around and I went in spirals through the air like a moth over to my sitting body and I flew round and round into the ear of that body and then was looking out of my eyes again back in my Boy-Body not Owl not Hound just Boy and I saw the lines of silver rain and felt the wetness all around and saw in a FLASH Drunkle and Rhiannon crawling towards me and Rhiannon's hands had all gone wrong and I could hear her screaming and so I gave a screaming back to them not their Names just the No-Word Noise which really *was* their Names and mine too and even Arrn's and everything on the World and the World itself that No-Word Noise was the Name of all and I made That Noise out there on top of the mountain in the wet words that the sky sent down yes I made that noise Just Me.

And then there were policemen and rooms and hospitals and doctors. People with pens asking me questions but not like them No Answer ones that grown-ups always give, no, these were Proper Questions which I *did* answer, yes. There was My Name on telly in the hospital room and My Mam Bethan was sitting at the end of the bed and she was crying. There was Drunkle too, a bandage wrapped round his head making him look like a desert feller. Where's your camel, Drunkle? There was Rhiannon in another bed in another part of the hospital and I went to see her and she was asleep and there were tubes going in her and her hands were wrapped in great big bandages like them big puffballs I find in the woods sometimes. There were pills I had to take and exercises I had to do and words I had to say and I said them. There was the finding of Arthur's body and the funeral when they put him back *in* the earth and I wondered why they didn't just leave him there down the hole and no one I knew went to that funeral not me or Drunkle or My Mam Bethan or even Rhiannon. There was the selling of Rhiannon's farm. There was the leaving of NotDad by My Mam Bethan and there was a big Coming Together at Drunkle's farm, me and Drunkle and Rhiannon and My Mam but no Arrn and there were lots of Crying Times and Talking Times in that big Coming Together in the farm on top of the mountain in those High Parts.

And that was last summer and this is this and the bluesome brightness is come again. Bala Lake is still on in my room but still no monster comes up out of it but right now I'm not looking at it anyway I'm looking out of the window down into the still clean yard and I can see Drunkle and My Mam Bethan moving the new sheep across the yard and I can see Rhiannon sitting on Straw Hill and she doesn't make me go Hot and Hard any more but she does make me go Warm cos I like her being on the planet and in a place where

I can see her even with her not-proper arms any more. I think a lot about when she touched me with the fingers she had then and doesn't any more and one of her arms is still in bandages the left one where it ends. I remember the Owl. Rhiannon is sitting on straw bales and the black-and-white cat is sitting by her and giving a smiling to the new sheep and he seems to like Rhiannon because he is always following her around the yard and sitting by her even tho she cannot stroke him properly. Later I will go out and talk to him like I do every night and he listens cos he can understand and I can hear him too and what he says. Rhiannon's daughter stays with us sometimes but today like most days she is in Swansea. This is what the world is now around me on these High Parts.

Drunkle looks up and sees me looking down and he waves at me and smiles. Even from up here I can see the bad mark on his head purple it is and big. I give a wave back to him and he calls me down so I go down there and look at Bala Lake a last time before I go but still there is no monster in that lake and so I turn it off.

And halfway down the stairs I hear it again; that voice from inside the mountain. Arrn it is, he's calling me. He doesn't sound lost and he doesn't sound sad he's just checking on me to see if I'm okay and at the same time telling me that *he's* okay and I hear his voice sometimes doing that and I hear it now so I sit down on the stairs to listen to it, his calling voice from inside the mountain, and I close my eyes and ears and nose and mouth and just listen to him calling my name and it's like just before My Times when everything leaves me and it's like I'm nothing just air, and in them few seconds when there is nothing in me but Arrn's voice or air I can't imagine, no, being anywhere else but here, on this High Place. I can't imagine being anyone else but Me and it makes me happy that does, so happy, more happy than I've ever been in my life since before I was born.

ACKNOWLEDGEMENTS

This book was written in Sweden. My thanks in that country to: Stefan, Anna and Marcus in Gothenburg; Birgitta Berglund, Anders, Malcolm, Ebba and Dante; Kiki Lindell; Sara Hakansson; Marianne and Axel Thormahlen; Claes Lindskog; Marie Wellin; Karin Altenberg; and anybody else I've forgotten in Lund, Malmö, Stockholm, Ales Stenar, Ystad and Helsingborg.